AT DARK OF THE MOON

Alice Chetwynd Ley

AT DARK OF THE MOON

Published by Sapere Books.

20 Windermere Drive, Leeds, England, LS17 7UZ,
United Kingdom

saperebooks.com

ISBN: 978-1-913028-31-2

ONE

That Spring and early Summer of 1804, England lay under the threat of an invasion from France. Across the Channel, Napoleon Bonaparte was marshalling his Grande Armée in readiness for his descent upon the people whom he had contemptuously called a nation of shopkeepers. His Iron Coast bristled with troops, while every French seaport and inland river town had been mobilised for building the vessels needed to convey these troops to England.

News of the preparations was carried across the Channel by the Americans and other neutrals, while rumour hastened to add colour to their reports. Some said a monster bridge was being built from Calais to Dover; others favoured a Channel tunnel — a terrifying thought to those who lived on the South Coast.

The London print shops, always quick to reflect the nation's mood, were stacked with pamphlets bearing titles such as "Ring the Alarum Bell!" or "Britons, to Arms!" Queen Elizabeth's speech at Tilbury and the Harfleur Lines from Shakespeare's Henry V were posted up on church doors or in market places. Alongside them appeared grim placards depicting the horrors of invasion for those without sufficient imagination to conjure up such dreadful scenes for themselves.

In the House of Commons, Mr. Pitt announced his plans for military defence — the raising of an additional Volunteer Force and the construction of Martello towers at intervals around the coast. Wide-eyed children in coastal areas watched beacons being built on hills once used by an earlier race of Britons as fortifications. They ran home to scolding mothers who threatened them with "Boney" if they did not do as they were told.

And everywhere, there was talk of spies. Some said that Napoleon himself, disguised as a British sailor, made periodic visits to lonely coves along the coast in a fishing boat. Inoffensive holiday-makers on the Isle of Thanet were arrested by the military because they were examining passing ships through perspective glasses — a completely innocent pastime, as it turned out.

But there were those whose activities were not so innocent.

Long before nightfall, the sky had been overcast; but now the clouds parted for a moment to allow the moon to make a brief appearance. By its pale, reluctant light, Bagshot Heath looked even more wild and desolate than by day. Heather, bracken and gorse sprawled like unkempt hair over its surface, divided here and there by narrow, stony tracks.

It was undulating country, in places dipping suddenly into great hollows that might have offered concealment to a small body of men. In one of these, close to the London to Southampton road which wound beside the Heath, white in the unexpected moonlight, two horsemen waited. Their faces were masked, their ears alert for the slightest sound.

"Devil take the moon!" muttered one. "They ought to be here by now, I reckon."

The other glanced up to where already clouds were again closing over the pale source of light, restoring the darkness which had been more welcome to these two sinister wayfarers.

"No matter — it's gone," replied the second man. "But if our quarry don't come soon, reckon I'll freeze to death." He slapped his hands against his sides, for the wind was sharp, although it was late in May. "I mislike this lay, too," he went on, "for all it's well salted. Nabbing purses and shiners is one thing as I understands, but papers and suchlike — who knows what a mort of trouble they could bring?" He broke off, cocking his head in the direction of the road. "Hsst! There's a coach now."

They waited a moment, ears straining. The other man nodded in the darkness as the clatter of wheels and hoofs grew louder. He leaned forward to loosen the pistols in their holsters.

"Now!" he commanded.

The loose stones went flying under their horses' hoofs as the riders spurred forward out of the hollow and on to the road right in the path of the oncoming coach.

"Stand and deliver!"

The postilion showed no disposition to argue but brought his team to a skidding halt; he did not consider his duties included acting like a hero in such circumstances. One of the highwaymen covered him with a pair of pistols, while the other dismounted and pulled open the door of the chaise.

He ducked just in time as a shot whistled over his head.

"Gimme that, y'bastard!"

He reached forward to wrench a pistol from the hand of the coach's sole occupant. The weapon gleamed in the light of the carriage lamps, and the highwayman chuckled appreciatively as he stuffed it into the capacious pocket of his frieze coat.

"A pretty toy — silver, eh? Hand over the rest and quick about it, if ye value yer life."

The occupant of the coach hesitated for a second, then, shrugging slightly, drew a purse from his pocket and tossed it on to the floor. If he had hoped to gain an advantage from this manoeuvre he was disappointed, for the highwayman scooped up the purse and transferred it to his pocket in one swift movement, his pistol never wavering. The next moment the traveller, who was only of slight build, found himself seized by his hefty attacker and dragged bodily from the coach to be dumped in the road beside the horses, where he was covered by the second man's pistols.

The first highwayman returned to the chaise and began to subject it to a thorough search. Having looked under the seat and thrown the cushions off, he turned his attention to the upholstery, prodding and poking. At last he gave an exclamation of satisfaction as a hinged section yielded under his fingers, revealing a small cubby-hole behind. He thrust in his hand, drawing out a packet wrapped in oilskin. He displayed it to his companion as he joined him on the road.

For the first time, the traveller betrayed some uneasiness as his eye fell on the packet in the highwayman's left hand.

"That's of no value to you," he said, quickly. "They're personal papers, no more. I have a gold snuff box here, and a diamond pin — take those, and leave me the package."

"We'll take those right enough, cully," grated the highwayman. "Hand 'em over, and no tricks, mind. I'm a nervous man on the trigger. Quick, now."

As he spoke, he moved the pistol in a warning gesture. The traveller produced the articles he had mentioned, offering them in fingers which trembled slightly. They were snatched from his grasp and stowed swiftly away. He kept his hand out expectantly. "The package," he said.

The highwayman whistled his horse, which had been standing quietly a few yards away, on the edge of the heath. It came obediently, evidently knowing its part in the night's business. He swung into the saddle.

"Well, now," he said. "Reckon if it's worth somethink to you, it could be to me."

"But you agreed —" The traveller broke off, evidently realising the hopelessness of expecting a felon to keep a bargain. "I'll pay you well for it," he said, earnestly. "I've no more money about me at present, but I'll undertake to send two hundred to any place you care to name within two days."

"Along the Runners, I s'pose?" replied the highwayman scornfully. "No, cully, ye can't catch an old hen with a piece o' straw. Tell you what, though," he added, with a wink, "since ye wants that packet so bad, ye might just chance to find it a fortnight hence at the pawnshop corner o' Stinking Lane. Prices is terrible high there, though. Cost ye double that, I reckon — but that's yer own look out. Take it or leave it."

The traveller's mouth twisted. It was no news to him that purloined possessions could sometimes be bought back by their owners at one of the many shady establishments in London's poor quarters. Such people were really fences, of course, but nothing could be done about them by the all too scanty forces of law and order. The unlawful trade was usually masked by a legitimate one; and what Bow St. Runner would willingly venture into those notorious rookeries unless for some more urgent purpose than to unite a gentleman with his gold snuff box?

He scarcely had time to complete these bitter reflections before the two highwaymen wheeled their horses and vanished into the blackness of the Heath. Over tracks known only to those few who were familiar with this wild place, they rode hard in the direction of Bagshot village. The Heath dwindled, and they took a narrow, rough lane which presently led past a pair of mean cottages where no light showed. Here they drew rein. One man entered the first of the cottages, while his companion led both horses round to some sheds at the rear, where someone was waiting to receive the animals. He then entered the same cottage by the back door.

Some time elapsed before the front door opened briefly and one of the men emerged. He had discarded his mask and frieze coat, though there was no one abroad in that lonely spot to observe the fact, even if the moon had given any light. Instead, he wore a well-cut greatcoat fashionably adorned with several capes.

He stepped out briskly, soon covering the mile or so to the village. There were few signs of life here, either, until he pushed open the door of the Three Mariners, where one or two countrymen were gathered in the tap room. He was evidently expected, for the landlord came over to him at once, nodding towards the back of the house. He went down a short, dark passage and tapped lightly on a door at the extreme end of it. A quiet voice bade him enter.

The man who was waiting there looked as if he had ridden hard just recently, for his well-cut riding dress still bore the stains of travel. He was of medium height, broad shouldered but not heavy and had a thin, intelligent face with keen brown eyes. He paused in the act of ladling some steaming punch into a tankard from a large bowl on the table.

"Ah, Freddie! The very man I was hoping to see — you've picked your moment well. Chilly night, ain't it? Draw up a chair to the fire, and I'll give you some of this. Just this minute been brought in, and smells devilish good, don't you think?"

The man addressed as Freddie loosened his topcoat and sank into a chair, stretching his long legs out towards the welcome blaze. He sniffed at the tankard proffered him, nodded approvingly, then took a gulp.

"As you say, Rupert, devilish good. Well, here's to the High Toby and Six String Jack, the old rogue — couldn't have brought it off without him!"

"You got what you wanted?"

"Easy as taking snuff, dear boy. That old villain Jack's a devilish enterprising customer, too. When our man offered to buy the packet back — just as we wanted, of course — Jack sends up the price in the wink of an eye to double the figure. Born to make his fortune, that one, if he don't end up on the Nubbing Cheat."

"Which is all too probable. Let's examine your haul, then."

Setting down his tankard, Freddie drew from his pocket the package which had been taken a few hours earlier from the luckless traveller. The other man took it, unfastened it with meticulous care, and spread out on the table several papers it contained. Freddie rose to join him in his close scrutiny of these.

"Gibberish!" exclaimed Freddie in disgust. "No sense that I can see in any of 'em."

"They're in cypher — no matter. We've an expert to deal with that and the necessary alterations to the text. Then our man in Grub Street will make a fair copy and Six String Jack's nefarious relative in Stinking Lane can sell them back to their owner. Neat, don't you agree?"

Freddie chuckled. "Devilish neat! Forgers and highwaymen — damned fine company we keep nowadays, m'boy! Still it's devilish fine sport, and more to my taste than doing the social round in Town, I'll allow."

"Sport, yes, but like all sports, attended by dangers," his companion reminded him, as he carefully replaced the papers in their packaging. "One must not quite forget that. Talking of the social round, that's what I shall shortly be doing next, if matters go as planned. But in Dorset, I must add, and not in London."

"Dorset, you say? But I thought you were too deep in this affair to be moved at present."

"It's all part of this affair. There have been suggestions in some of the intercepted documents that the villages east of Weymouth would repay investigation. Rumour has it that King George is far from well at present, but it may be that he'll make the annual visit to Weymouth as usual later in the Summer. A great deal will be going on there — by all reports, a great deal is going on already. If an invasion is possible, the two most likely points are in Dorset or farther to the West. I am instructed that my presence is needed — the man there is called Abney and can be relied upon."

"Devil take it! Do I go with you?"

"Can't say, at present. Plans are still in the melting pot. It seems I'm to have a companion though — a wife."

Freddie stared, aghast. "A *wife!* Hell and the devil, man, I'd no notion you were so much as betrothed! Wish you happy and all that, of course," he added, belatedly. "Who's it to be — anyone I'm acquainted with?"

There was a twinkle in the other's eye. He shook his head. "I fear I can't enlighten you. I'm not yet acquainted with the lady myself."

"Not —!" Freddie made a choking sound. "Well, damme if that don't beat all!"

TWO

Although the schoolroom at Marton Hall could never have been considered an attractive apartment, Miss Harcourt usually chose to spend her lonely evenings sitting there. Her austere bedchamber offered the only alternative, and she found something melancholy in retiring to it immediately after dinner was over. Unfortunately, the arrangements made by the mistress of the house for her daughters' governess took no account of this point of view. Mrs. Bowyer was a woman who believed in having her pound of flesh, and she considered that already Miss Harcourt had the better of their contract. Was the governess not paid fifteen pounds annually for her services, fed at their own table, and housed in a bedchamber of ample proportions, even if this did happen to be up a rather dark little stairway at the back of the house? Moreover, it was not even as if the young woman had been highly qualified for the post. One of Mrs. Bowyer's acquaintances had in her employ a governess who could teach Italian as well as French, and who spent most of her time in training her charges in what Mrs. Bowyer thought of as the little elegancies, rather than in stuffing their heads with useless nonsense about history and literature and such like. And as Miss Harcourt had been unable to furnish any references beyond a letter from a schoolmistress now living retired in Cumberland, it had really been an act of charity for Mrs. Bowyer to take her on at all.

Miss Harcourt was never left in any doubt of her employer's attitude towards her; but, all the same, she did realise that she was fortunate to have any post that enabled her to earn a living, however meagre. Since her father's untimely death, there had been no one to provide for her. Nevertheless, it was ironical that anyone should be obliged to think herself fortunate to be working in such a household as this, and for such a woman.

She laid aside her book for a moment and sighed, allowing her thoughts to wander. Would her life always be like this, she wondered? When the Bowyer children grew too old for her instruction, others would take their place — that was, if she chanced to find new teaching posts at all — and the process would continue, until she herself was too old to pursue it any longer. And afterwards? She shuddered as the long vista of years opened up before her, grey and cheerless as a winter sky.

She shook off the momentary depression, ashamed of herself for indulging it. Her father had taught her that, though life undoubtedly had its ups and downs, there was always the chance of a fair prospect over the brow of the hill. Remembering Major George Harcourt, who had died gallantly with General Abercromby in Egypt three years ago, a tender smile touched her lips. It was still there when the schoolroom door opened softly, and a young man tiptoed in, closing it with exaggerated care.

He was handsome in a florid kind of way and wore a complacent air which suggested that he was well aware of the fact. He approached Miss Harcourt with an ingratiating smile which set her teeth on edge.

"Ah," he said, in tones of satisfaction. "I was hoping I might find you here."

The smile left her face. "What do you want?" she demanded, uncompromisingly.

"Not a very civil greeting, Emma."

"I've yet to learn that I made you free of my name," she snapped.

"Oh, come, my dear." He moved behind her chair and leaned over the back of it to place his hands on her shoulders. "You surely can't be so cruel when I've made it plain that I admire you vastly."

She wriggled free of his grasp, leaping to her feet. "And I thought I'd made it equally plain that I don't wish for your attentions!"

"Maidenly modesty," he scoffed. "But there's no need to carry it to extremes, dearest girl — we're quite alone now."

"Precisely. I *am* alone — and unprotected. Can you think it right to take advantage of my situation in this way?"

"You need not be either." He moved from behind the chair to stand facing her. "I am more than willing to be your protector, my love. I could take a house for you — at a discreet distance from here, of course," he added quickly. "I would give you everything that your beauty and charm deserve. No more drudging away your youth in trying to knock some learning into my idle brats of sisters — we'd have a rare old time of it, you and I. What d'you say, dearest Emma?"

While she stood speechless, her colour coming and going, he made a sudden grab at her that knocked her off balance. Before she could recover, his arms had closed about her violently, and she fell backwards into the chair, dragging him with her.

At that moment the door was thrust open and Mrs. Bowyer herself burst into the room. Her more than generous bosom quivered with indignation at the sight that met her eyes, threatening to burst the bounds of her low-cut evening gown.

"Just as I thought!" she exclaimed, with mingled satisfaction and disgust. "I heard something going on, and not for the first time, I'll warrant, you trollop, you! As for you, Tom, get up this minute!"

The young man extricated himself, looking sheepish. Miss Harcourt also rose to her feet, her face pale and set.

"Outside!" Mrs. Bowyer instructed her son, in strident tones from which all traces of her usual superimposed genteel accent were missing. "I'll deal with you later, my boy!"

Tom made his exit rapidly, watched in silent scorn by his mother. When the door had closed upon him, she turned the full battery of her ire on the unfortunate governess. Not stopping to choose her terms, which would have done credit to a Billingsgate fishwife, she upbraided Miss Harcourt for worming her way into a genteel household with the object of entrapping a credulous young man into marriage.

"Believe me, madam," put in Miss Harcourt, when her employer paused momentarily for breath, "I would not for one moment entertain the notion of accepting Mr. Thomas Bowyer, even if the offer he had made me had been an honourable one."

"Oh, so my son's not good enough for you, you hussy, is that it?" shouted Mrs. Bowyer, changing course rapidly. "Hoping for a better catch, are you? Well you'll not set about it with my help, let me tell you, you whey-faced bitch, for I'll give you no recommendation when you leave my roof — and that will be this instant, so you'd best pack your belongings straight away, or else I'll throw them after you into the street, see if I don't!"

Miss Harcourt was very pale now, but she stood her ground. "This is the grossest injustice, madam! Your son came here uninvited to persecute me with gallantries which I neither sought nor desired — and not for the first time, I may add! I would have asked you to interfere before this, but I feared it would result in my dismissal, and I hoped that he might lose interest if I consistently repulsed him. But to be turned off at a moment's notice in this way for something which is my misfortune rather than my fault — and at this hour of the night, too! Where do you suppose I can go?"

"Women of your sort can always find themselves a bed," replied Mrs. Bowyer with an unpleasant laugh. "Besides, what do I care where you go, you whore, so long as I'm shot of you? Twenty minutes I'll give you, no more, to get out — and I'll see you off the premises in person, so don't think you can sneak in again when my back's turned."

Miss Harcourt swallowed and raised her head with a tattered dignity which might have aroused compassion in a woman of finer feelings than Mrs. Bowyer. "Very well, madam. But I shall be obliged to leave some of my possessions for collection later — there are books for instance which are too heavy for me to take now. I — I trust you will have no objection to that?"

"Well, you'd best send for them quickly, then, or I'll have them thrown out. You can't expect that I'll keep your rubbish about for ever. I shall be needing your room for the next governess. And I warn you that I'll be looking over anything you leave behind — who knows what you might help yourself to, otherwise? Off you go now and make haste. Twenty minutes I said, and that's all you'll get before I have you thrown out, packed or no."

Miss Harcourt obediently went from the room and made her way upstairs as quickly as a sudden weakness in her limbs permitted. She pushed the door of her room open with a trembling hand and then stood still for a brief moment while she took two or three breaths to steady herself. She was certainly not the type to fall into a hysterical swoon, but a good cry now would have done much to relieve her feelings.

There was no time. Undoubtedly that dreadful woman meant what she said. Bracing herself, Miss Harcourt took a carpet bag from one of the cupboards and began methodically to pack it with the scanty contents of her wardrobe, some toilet articles and her few most treasured personal possessions. Little remained other than her books; these she packed into a trunk with as much care as time would permit, leaving the trunk unfastened so that Mrs. Bowyer might satisfy herself that it contained nothing that did not belong to its owner.

She had barely finished when she heard a tap on the door and, opening it, saw one of the manservants standing outside.

"Madam says you're to come, Miss," he said loudly; then, lowering his tone, "It's a blamed shame, Miss — I know that randy young devil's ways. If you'll wait by the gate outside, Miss, I'll get word to Jim to sneak the gig out o' the stables and drive you down to the Crown in the village, where you're sure to get a bed, and there'll be a stage through in the morning."

The tears which had been held back in adversity came to her eyes at this unlooked-for kindness. "Oh, thank you! But I wouldn't for the world get Jim into trouble — do you think he should?"

He nodded reassuringly. "Stable's far enough from the house, and he'll go the back way. Never fear, Miss — and good luck."

She began to thank him again but was interrupted by a shout from downstairs. Giving her a warning look, he swung up the carpet bag and dashed down the stairs to the hall, leaving her to follow at a more leisurely pace. When she reached the hall, Mrs. Bowyer was waiting and lost no time in seeing her off the premises, closing the door behind her with a resounding slam.

It sounded like a knell in Miss Harcourt's ears. She had no idea where she could go, friendless as she was in this part of the country. She must sleep tonight at the Crown, as the kindly footman had suggested, and then tomorrow she supposed she had better make for London, where there were employment agencies. She must find another post quickly, for it was certain that she could not subsist long on what remained in her purse of her slender salary.

Fortunately, there was a moon tonight, so she had no difficulty in finding her way round to the stables without the aid of a lantern. When she reached there, she found Jim harnessing the horse to the gig. She breathed a deep sigh of relief. It was more than a mile to the village, and her bag was heavy. He helped her up, and soon they had left her late employer's house behind and were setting a spanking pace along the road which led to the village.

When the first cottages came into sight, Jim drew rein.

"You'll not mind, Miss, but I'd leifer not draw up outside the Crown, beggin' y'r pardon. They know me there and if Missus should get to hear of it, I'd likely lose my place, as well. So I'll set ye down here, though sorry I am to do it, seeing as ye've baggage to manage."

"I don't regard that in the least," replied Emma Harcourt, feeling a little better now, in spite of all her difficulties. "You've been so kind, I wouldn't for the world get you into trouble, and it's only a step to the inn.'

He helped her out of the gig and handed her the bag. She set it down for a moment, extending her hand to him. "Goodbye, Jim, and thank you."

He looked at her hand doubtfully for a moment, then wiped his own on his breeches before taking it. "Goodbye, Miss Harcourt, ma'am. Ye were the only real lady in that house, danged if ye weren't."

He turned away as though ashamed of this minor outburst, and, wheeling the gig, drove off with a backward wave. Feeling as though she had lost her only friend, Emma Harcourt returned the salutation, then took up her bag and started towards the inn.

In less than five minutes, she was standing in the entrance hall. The landlord came forward, looking her over with a shrewd eye, which did not miss the lack of fashion in her attire, nor the fact that she appeared to have arrived on foot and unattended. She asked for a room. He shook his head, at first doubtfully, then more decisively as he finally recognised her for the governess from the Hall. He quickly guessed that there had been some trouble and had no wish to involve himself in it. The Bowyers were good customers, and he was not the man to disoblige clients for the sake of an insignificant Miss without a penny to her name.

"Oh, but, please!" she pleaded in dismay. "Where can I go? There is nowhere else near at hand."

A youngish woman who was passing through the hall at that moment overheard the words and paused, struck by the note of panic in the otherwise pleasant voice. Voices were a part of her profession, and always the first thing she noticed about anyone. She studied the new arrival surreptitiously, finding little difficulty in guessing what her profession was, but having a lively curiosity about how the young woman came to be here at this hour of the night trying to book a room, and sounding very desperate about it.

"I can't say, I'm sure," answered the landlord with a shrug. "All I know is I'm full up."

"But — but I'll sleep *anywhere*," persisted Miss Harcourt, earnestly. "It is only for tonight — a chair before the kitchen fire will do, if you can offer nothing better."

"I've told you once, I can't offer anything," replied the landlord, with a snap. "That's the end of the matter, as far as I'm concerned."

Miss Harcourt's face was very pale now, but she showed no other sign of her inward trepidation as she bent to pick up her luggage.

"Just a moment, ma'am." The other woman came forward and laid a detaining hand upon Miss Harcourt's arm. "If you shouldn't object to sharing a room with me, there is an unoccupied bed in my chamber. I promise you —" she flashed a warm smile at the governess — "that I don't snore."

Surprise and gratitude flooded the drawn face. "Oh, how very kind! I — I just don't know how to thank you, ma'am!"

"Wait a bit," put in the landlord, truculently. "You ladies are settling all without consulting my convenience. And what I says is —"

"Come now!" Emma's rescuer turned the warmth of her smile upon him, together with a cajoling look from a very fine pair of hazel eyes; "What possible harm can it do you, landlord, to gain two fees instead of one for my room?"

He felt the force of this argument but would not give in too readily. "There's the bed to make up," he grumbled, "and all the maids gone home — my Missus won't thank me."

"I am persuaded your good wife will find it the work of a moment," replied his guest, not scrupling to add flattery to cajolery. "One has only to be an hour or two in your hostelry to realise that the housekeeping is of an unusually high standard."

The compliment, blatant though it was, obviously had a softening effect. Muttering something about going to consult his wife, he disappeared down the passage leading to the back quarters. The lady's dignified air dropped away from her and she giggled like a schoolgirl.

"Oh, my dear! I really think we have carried the day!"

"I can only hope so, ma'am, for I don't mind telling you that my case is desperate. If I can't take advantage of your most generous offer, I cannot think what to do," said Miss Harcourt, despondently.

"So I guessed," replied the other, quietly. "And as I've frequently been in a tight corner myself, you had my complete sympathy. But here he comes."

Evidently, the landlord's wife had raised no serious objection, for he informed them that the spare bed would be made up immediately, and the room ready in about a quarter of an hour.

Miss Harcourt readily fell in with her new-found friend's suggestion that, in the meantime, a hot beverage might not come amiss; and as the landlord assured them that the coffee room was empty at present, they settled down there comfortably together.

Emma Harcourt now had time to take stock of her companion. She judged that the other young woman was perhaps four years older than herself. She was a little taller than Emma and more generously made, though her figure was well proportioned. Her blonde hair was attractively dressed in a top knot with ringlets dangling from it, her complexion was creamy, her mouth wide and generous, and her hazel eyes were most expressive. She had an air of confident nonchalance which suggested, thought Emma, that she had mixed a good deal in the world with people of every kind. Although she was fashionably dressed, she wore her clothes with a careless grace which seemed typical of her. Her manner was easy and informal, offering a shortcut to friendship.

"We'd better introduce ourselves, since we're to be bedfellows," she said, with a laugh. "I'm Antonia Maleverer — but it's not my real name, of course. Still, I've become accustomed to it through years of use. You can call me Toni, if you like — most people do."

"I — I beg your pardon? Did you say not your real name?"

"Oh, how stupid of me! I'm forgetting you don't know I'm an actress. Not that anyone's ever heard of me," she added, candidly, "more's the pity. I'm not what you might call a *succès fou* — in fact, to be honest with you, I'm more or less a failure."

"I can sympathise — I seem to be somewhat of a failure myself. I'm Emma Harcourt, by the way, and I am — or perhaps I should say I was until this evening — a governess."

"Oh, yes, I'd guessed that," replied Antonia, in a lively tone. "And I must confess I'm all curiosity as to why you ceased to be one this evening! But I mustn't force your confidence," she added, in response to the guard that came over Emma's face. "Pray don't take any notice of me — I mean no harm, but I do go on, you know."

The grey eyes softened. "Your words are a well merited reproach to me, ma'am. After such kindness as yours, the least I can do is to explain how I come to be in my present plight."

"Well, I think it will do you good to talk about it, anyway," said Antonia. "But pray don't call me 'ma'am' — I feel as if I had offended you! Antonia or Toni, just as you please."

"Very well, Toni," said Emma, after just the slightest hesitation. "You see, it was like this."

She recounted the circumstances of her dismissal. Antonia heard her out in a sympathetic silence.

"You poor dear!" she said, at the end. "It's a most uncomfortable business to have attentions forced on one by an employer — I myself have suffered, and one way or another, it nearly always ends in having to find another place. So what do you intend doing now?"

Emma shrugged helplessly. "I shall take the stage from here in the morning to London and hope to find something at one of the agencies. But the only recommendation I possess isn't a very strong one, I fear, as it was written more than two years since, by my old schoolmistress. It would be worse than useless to refer a prospective employer to Mrs. Bowyer, so I can naturally make no mention of my teaching there. Still," she continued, resolutely, "there must be something I can find, even if it is only as a companion to an elderly lady."

Antonia shook her head. "Oh, dear, I've been through all this myself so many times! And I must say — though I don't want to dishearten you, my dear — that I've always found agencies little better than broken reeds to depend upon! They take so long to find one employment; and, even when they do, it's rarely suitable, for one reason or another. Have you no friends who could help you to find another post? Or relatives with whom you could stay while you look about for something of your own choosing?"

"No one I wish to approach," replied Emma, firmly. "No, I must stand on my own feet, neither can I afford to wait any length of time for a post. I must take whatever offers and make the best of it until something more suitable turns up."

The other looked at her consideringly for a few moments. "I wonder — but, no, of course it would not do for you."

"What wouldn't do for me?" asked Emma, with lively interest. "Believe me, I'll be grateful for any suggestions! My present position is such that I would consider almost anything."

"Oh, well, if you mean that," began Antonia, then broke off. "But I don't suppose it would be any use at all, for I dare say you've never done any acting in your life, have you?"

"*Acting?*" Emma's voice rose a little on the word. "Do you mean on the *stage?*"

Antonia nodded.

"Why, no, not unless you count a few amateur theatrical performances when I was a pupil at a Seminary. But that's a very long time ago, in any case," she added.

"How good were you?" demanded the other. "No false modesty, now, for a great deal may depend on your answering truthfully."

"I don't really know," replied Emma, slowly. "Everyone said at the time that I was very good — but they would, you know, because they were my teachers, relatives and friends, after all. I'm quite sure a true professional such as yourself would have found me painfully inadequate."

"I don't know." The actress considered her thoughtfully. "You've a good, clear voice; and I've seen for myself that you're able to conceal your true feelings quite successfully. It's only a small step from that to being able to portray imagined ones. As a governess, I dare say you'd be obliged to play a part most of the time — and I feel reasonably sure that the Madam Prunes and Prisms role you've set yourself has been foreign to your true nature. After all, they only want someone for *amateur* theatricals. That's what I was told."

"You mean you know of a post for me as — as an amateur actress?" asked Emma incredulously.

"Yes, my dear, I do. And I believe it would be the very thing for you," said Antonia, warming to her theme, "as it is only for three months, which would give you time to look about you for something in your own line, you know. At least, it would mean that you needn't starve in the meantime."

"You — you are very good," said Emma faintly. "But to give public performances — no, I fear I am not equal to it."

"No, no, not *public* performances — didn't I tell you it was for private theatricals? You would only be expected to perform in a private house before a small group of people — a family affair, with some members of the family taking part with you. You know how addicted to private theatricals many members of the upper classes are at present." She shook her head. "Still, never mind. Perhaps it would not do for you, only I thought you were desperate; and, truth to tell, it would serve me a good turn, too. However, that is nothing. Perhaps I can think of something else to help you."

Emma set her mouth in a firm line. "No, you are quite right, I *am* desperate. I — I have very little money, you see, and certainly can't afford to reject anything at present. Tell me more about this."

"Well. I'll tell you what I know, but that's precious little. The fact is, I accepted this engagement for myself some months ago when I needed something badly, just as you do now. Only now I don't need it. Indeed, I'd be glad to get out of the obligation, as I've recently been offered a more or less permanent position with a very good touring company where I have friends. But one can't let people down in my way of business, you know, so I was prepared to go on with this for the time stipulated and join the Company afterwards. They *said* it would be all right, but one never knows, you see," she finished, doubtfully. "I'd far rather go to them straight away, for fear they change their minds and take on someone else."

"And if I were to take up this earlier appointment in your place, it would leave you free, of course?"

Antonia nodded.

"Yes, I do see that it might be advantageous to both of us, but what of the people who engaged you? Do you suppose,"

Emma asked doubtfully, "that they would be at all willing to accept me in your stead? Who are they?"

"That I can't say, for I never heard their name mentioned. I was interviewed in London by an elderly lady of the first elegance — quite the *grande dame* manner, I assure you, my dear! I was almost too overcome to answer her questions, let alone ask many myself! I must say that the questions she did ask were a little out of the common way. She seemed more concerned with my character and background than with my acting ability — she seemed particularly anxious to know whether I had ever appeared in Dorset or had any connections of any kind there. I supposed at the time that she wished to make sure I wasn't an undesirable type of female, as I was to be admitted to a family circle obviously of some standing. But the references to Dorset I couldn't at all understand, I must confess."

"Well," said Emma, gloomily, "I must say that it doesn't sound as if they would be willing to accept me as a substitute for you. I certainly shan't be given a good character by my late employer, and these people are sure to want to know how I have been employed over the past few years. And who is there to vouch for my acting ability?"

"You're quite right, my love. That had already occurred to me as a difficulty," replied Antonia, calmly. "And that's why I don't propose to enlighten them about the substitution. You must begin your acting career by posing as me."

THREE

"But — but I couldn't possibly do that!" Emma was aghast. "Such duplicity — no, I cannot entertain the idea for a moment!"

"All acting is a form of duplicity," said Antonia Maleverer, reasonably.

"One accepts that, of course, on the stage. But in real life — no, I couldn't sleep easy in my bed!"

"At least you'd have a bed to sleep in," the other reminded her, quietly. "Besides, what real harm would you be doing by the deception? I'm quite sure you would do your best to fulfil the terms of your contract."

"Indeed I should, but my best couldn't possibly compare to yours, Toni. And since I'm to pass myself off as you, I would be laying claim to a competence I don't possess. Oh!" she broke off suddenly, and some of the worry went out of her expression — "I have just thought! I couldn't possibly pretend to be you, in any event, for the lady whom you met in London would know at once that I was an impostor."

"Oh, my dear, pray, credit me with a little intelligence! Naturally, I wouldn't have suggested the scheme had there been the slightest likelihood of your meeting her. She told me quite distinctly that she was acting on behalf of friends who were unable to be in London at that time, but that she would not be one of the country house party, so I needn't expect to see her again."

"Did she say in what part of the country? Was it somewhere here in Hampshire?"

"Why, no; but she instructed me to come here to this inn, where a room would be taken for me for one night, and that on the following morning (tomorrow, that is) a private coach would arrive to take me to my ultimate destination."

"But surely she told you where it is?"

"Well, no. As a matter of fact, I didn't trouble to ask. It's all one to me where I go, so long as I am well paid to go there," said Antonia, carelessly.

"But surely it is very strange not to be told either your destination or the name of your employers? Or are such arrangements usual in your profession?"

"Not to say usual, but one takes what offers, you know. I'm a competent enough actress in my own style, but I'm no Sarah Siddons, my dear, and I can't afford to pick and choose! Few of us can, when penury is the alternative, and I was desperate enough for employment at that particular time."

"As I am now," said Emma glumly. She brooded in silence for a few minutes, then burst out — "I wish I knew what to do! I mislike this scheme — and I don't care to be obliged to deceive anyone. And yet, what else is there for me to do?"

Antonia put a sympathetic hand on her arm. "I mustn't persuade you, for your scruples do you credit; but in your place I wouldn't hesitate. You're in the devil of a coil, you know. Maybe you've never before been without a roof over your head and the price of a meal, but I have, and I can tell you it don't encourage one to have scruples! Besides, you know, they need not keep you on if you fail to give satisfaction."

"Should I decide to undertake this venture," replied Emma, with a determined lift of her chin, "I shall use every endeavour to make sure that I *do* give satisfaction. But you are right, of course. They would not be under any obligation to me. All the same —" her voice wavered — "I do so hate to practise any kind of deception."

"When a female has to shift for herself in the world, she must learn the art of compromise," Antonia said philosophically. "But you must do what you think best. Why not sleep on it, my dear? You have until the morning to decide, and things often look clearer by daylight, in more senses than one."

The advice seemed good, so they said no more on the subject, and very soon retired for the night.

Antonia was soon asleep, but Emma lay awake for most of the night, uneasy thoughts going around and round in her mind. Even if she found herself the cheapest possible lodging in London, in a respectable quarter, her slender means would not support her for more than a fortnight. Could she possibly rely upon finding another post in that short space of time, especially without a recent recommendation? There was always a plentiful supply of well qualified young — and not so young — women with excellent references, eager to present themselves for every advertised post as a governess. What was to become of her if she failed to secure one before her money had run out?

She told herself passionately that she would never go back to the house of her shrewish Aunt Caroline, where she had been made so miserable after her father's death. She had been treated there as an object of charity and had decided that it was preferable to earn her own living, even in a household such as the one she had just been obliged to quit.

Three months, Antonia had said. In three months, she had a much better chance of finding something, as the actress had pointed out. It would give her a breathing space. And yet — to be acting a part in one's daily life, to be set on a course of deliberate deception —

She dropped off at last into a brief slumber just as the birds were announcing a new day.

She awoke heavy-eyed, but resolute. She would grasp at the chance which was offered her. She communicated her decision to Antonia over breakfast in the coffee room.

"I shall make the attempt, at any rate," she said, determinedly. "But if they appear dissatisfied with my performance, I shall confess the whole. I feel I must warn you of this, in case it makes any difference to you. After all your kindness, the last thing I want to do is to place you in an awkward position. If you now feel that you wish to withdraw your generous offer, I assure you I shall quite understand."

Antonia laughed. "Lud, no, my dear! One mustn't take these things too seriously, after all. I couldn't bring myself to let them down completely, but as long as I've provided a substitute, I think myself quit of the obligation. If they don't find you suitable, they have their remedy. And now we must discuss business matters, don't you think? My fare from London was paid, and my lodging here. These are expenses they would have incurred for you, had you truly been in my shoes. I think it right, therefore, for me to pay your reckoning at the inn, as some kind of recompense to you."

Emma was by no means ready to accept this offer, but she found her friend surprisingly obstinate.

"Don't be thinking, Emma, that you're the only one with a conscience," she said, laughing. "Now, pray don't argue any more, for my mind is quite made up! I'm tolerably plump in the pocket, at present, and have better prospects in view than I've seen for many a long day."

Emma saw that it would hurt Antonia's feelings if any further objections were raised, so she accepted gratefully and changed the subject by asking at what time Antonia was expecting the coach which was to be sent for her.

"Eleven o'clock," replied Antonia, consulting the clock. "And as it's only just after nine, we've plenty of time to do your packing."

"Oh!" Emma jumped, as a sudden thought struck her. "What shall I do about the trunk I was obliged to leave at Marton Hall? I can't leave it there for three months, as Mrs. Bowyer threatened to throw it out if I didn't send for it as soon as possible."

"Send for it now. You can have it brought here within the hour, if we ask the landlord to see to it straight away, and then it can go with you in the coach."

"Do you think he would oblige?" asked Emma, doubtfully. "He didn't seem disposed to do me any favours last night."

"Leave it to me," said Antonia, with an unladylike wink. "I'll soon bring him round my thumb, see if I don't."

She departed on this errand, returning in a few minutes to say that the matter was successfully arranged. The two then returned to their bedchamber.

"Are these all the gowns you have?" asked Antonia, as she helped Emma to pack.

"Except for one or two warmer ones, which are in my trunk. I did not bring them with me as I didn't expect to need them at this season, and I had to travel light."

"But they are all like this?" insisted Antonia.

Emma wrinkled her brow. "What do you mean?"

"Why, don't be offended at me, but they are all so prodigiously — well — school-ma'amly!"

"What do you expect? That was my profession and you can't suppose that my late employer would have encouraged me to look like a fashion plate — even if I could have afforded to do so."

Antonia looked at her thoughtfully. "No, I can see that you did your best to appear older and more staid than you really are."

"I am almost three and twenty — quite old, you know."

Antonia laughed. "I can give you four years. But a female is as old as she looks, don't you agree? You've been playing the role of schoolmistress, Emma — you see, there's more of the actress in you than you will allow! But you can slough off that skin now, my dear, and I tell you plainly that these gowns won't help you to do it. Neither will that style of dressing your hair — it's a disaster! Come here and let me try what I can do to improve it. I'll wager we'll knock three or four years off your age in no time, and make you look more fitted to your new role."

"But I don't want to appear too juvenile, do I?" Emma objected. "Else your — my — employers will never believe I have any acting experience at all."

"They will be more likely to accept you as an actress if you look more the part. Did I not tell you that I guessed as soon as I set eyes on you what your profession must be? Come, let's see what we can do! It will serve to occupy the time until the coach comes for you."

"Oh, very well, since you think it advisable. I must confess that I adopted this style of dressing my hair because I felt it would make me look older, and not because I prefer it." She went to sit before the dressing table and began slowly to remove the pins from her hair. "In fact," she admitted, with a grimace in the mirror, "I positively detest it!"

"That's the spirit," approved Antonia, as she seized a brush. "Now for the transformation scene!"

Almost half an hour had elapsed before she was satisfied with her handiwork. She stepped back a little, to give one last, appraising look, before demanding what Emma thought of it.

Miss Harcourt stared at her reflection in the mirror. Could this really be the same girl who had looked back at her for the past few years? The oval, small featured face was the same, certainly; but this softly curling framework of gold-brown hair had altered it in some subtle way, making it less withdrawn and cold. Her eyes danced with mischief for a moment, changing the cool grey to a warmer blue shade.

"Capital!" applauded Antonia. "You shall go to the ball, Cinderella, but not — oh, not — in that gown!"

Emma stood up, smoothing a hand along the skirt of her fawn gown. "Why, what is wrong with it?"

"Everything!" replied the other, candidly. "Just as I have told you already, it's too staid and severe. Now, what can be done about it?"

"You don't prefer one of the others?" asked Emma, dubiously.

Antonia shook her head vigorously. "No, they are all impossible! I have it! I'll lend you one of mine! I know the very thing — it shrank a little when it was laundered, and I dare say it will fit you to perfection. Only wait till I find it!"

With one of her quick, impetuous movements she turned to a trunk which was lying beside her bed and flung back the lid. After a moment's search, she drew out a white muslin gown embroidered with small pink flowers, and holding it against Emma, turned her towards the mirror.

"There — does it not become you extremely?"

Emma looked, sighed, then gently pushed the gown away. "Oh, no, I couldn't — indeed I couldn't, Toni!" There were tears in her eyes and her voice trembled. "You are so good — I don't know when I've ever met anyone so good, and already you've done so much for one who is a perfect stranger. But I refuse to take the very clothes from your back!"

"Fustian! What a piece of work you're making over a very little thing, my dear! I had as lief be rid of this gown as not, for I'm quite tired of it. Besides that, it is far too small. So say no more but get into it directly."

But this Emma would by no means do, and they argued for some time.

"It's quite enough that I should borrow your identity, Toni," finished Emma, firmly. "And as I'll be wearing costume, I suppose, for my performance, it surely can't signify what I wear for the rest of the time. But I'll keep my hair like this," she conceded, in a gentler tone. "It reminds me of past times, when my father was alive."

"Are both your parents dead?" asked Antonia, momentarily diverted.

"Yes, my mother died when I was quite young. My father was an Army man and was killed in action three years ago."

"So you're alone in the world, like myself. Well, we must shift as best we can, my dear, and not feel sorry for ourselves, for I dare say there are plenty worse off. Now, do at least try on this wretched gown, just to please me! If it should fit you, it will help to create a good first impression, and that's a great deal, you know, in such matters."

To save further argument, Emma put on the gown, and had to admit that it was a great improvement. Antonia once more began to urge her to accept it, so at last she weakened sufficiently to say that she would borrow it for the time being.

"You must tell me where I can find you at the end of this engagement, Toni, and then I'll either send it back or bring it myself, whichever suits you best."

"Oh, very well, since at least it will give me an excuse for seeing you again. But I don't rightly know where I'll be in three months' time. I'll tell you what, though — I'll give you the direction of my old dresser in London. She was with me in the days when my father had his own touring company, and she's the one person who always knows where I may be found, for I never neglect writing, or seeing her as often as I can."

She was groping in the trunk again, and presently found a small leather folder from which she drew a letter. She tore off the top and gave it to Emma, who placed it in her reticule.

"There, now, perhaps you'll consent to keep the gown on — I must say it becomes you extremely, besides making you look much more like a member of the artistic profession." She paused as a tap came at the door. "Come in!"

It was one of the maids to say that the trunk had been fetched from Marton Hall and was waiting downstairs. She asked if it should be brought up, but Antonia told her to leave it where it was at present.

"Gracious, look at the time!" she exclaimed when the girl had gone. "It's turned a quarter to eleven! You'd best make ready."

Emma became aware of an unpleasant sinking sensation in the pit of her stomach. She sat down suddenly. "I am ready," she said, uncertainly, "except for my bonnet and gloves."

"Your bonnet!" exclaimed Antonia, seizing it and holding it up for inspection. "No, it is not too bad — a pity the ribbons aren't pink, but there's no time to change them now. We must just make the best of it, I suppose. Here, put it on."

Emma took it from her and tried to do so, but she found to her shame that her fingers were trembling too much to fasten the ribbons.

"Let me!" Antonia deftly tied a jaunty bow under Emma's chin. "First night nerves, you know," she said encouragingly. "You'll be all right on stage, I assure you."

"I shall have to be," replied Emma, tilting her chin. "Oh, Toni, there's so much I want to say to you — how can I ever begin to thank you for all your kindness — and I was a complete stranger! How I should have fared but for you I can't imagine!"

"Stuff! But you must look me out again — not just to return that stupid gown, but to give me the pleasure of seeing you! We've dealt famously together, don't you think? Almost as if we were sisters."

"Indeed, no sister could have done more for me! And I shall certainly come to see you, as soon as I'm free of this engagement — which might be sooner than we think," she added, gloomily.

Antonia was about to make a cheering reply, but the maid knocked again, this time to say that a private coach was down in the yard and the driver asking for Miss Maleverer.

"Your cue," said Antonia, giving Emma's carpet bag to the girl and sending her ahead. "I think it best if I don't come down, my dear. Au revoir and remember that you are now Antonia Maleverer, an actress. I wish you luck."

Emma nodded and swallowed. "Goodbye, Toni," she said, holding out her hand.

Then suddenly she flung her arms round Antonia, and for a moment they clung together like the sisters they might have been. Emma's eyes were wet as she disengaged herself and, straightening her bonnet, she marched resolutely on her fate.

FOUR

The coach took the road to Lyndhurst, but after about three miles it turned along a narrow lane which wound for mile after mile deep into the forest. At any other time, Emma would have enjoyed the drive, through sunlight-dappled trees with an occasional glimpse of deer flitting about in the distance. But in her present uneasy frame of mind, the scenes through which she was passing made no real impact on her senses. Every nerve in her body was tensed ready to meet the ordeal which lay ahead.

Once an almost uncontrollable impulse seized her to lower the window and shout to the coachman to stop, to take her back to the inn. It was still not too late to change her mind and retreat from this rash venture. She fought down the rising panic. What use was there now in going back? She had wrestled with the problem through most of the night and had reached a decision which both she and Antonia thought the best in the circumstances. Now she must summon to her aid all her resolution and wit in carrying it through.

She succeeded with difficulty in banishing these fears, only to find another kind of unease growing on her. The woods were thick about them on every side, with no sign of human habitation. It was as if some vast green giant had swallowed the coach whole, severing its occupant from the outside world for ever. As each bend in the track took them deeper into the forest, the feeling became worse. Where was the coach taking her? It would have been a considerable comfort to know exactly where she was bound, to have been told the name of the house or the village. As it was, she did not even know the name of her employer. Surely there must be something sinister about so mysterious an arrangement?

She reminded herself that Antonia, who had experience of accepting acting engagements, seemed to regard the terms of this one as nothing so very out of the way. Besides, beggars could not be choosers.

The homily did little to banish her apprehension. The only benefit — and it was a doubtful one — was that one fear had succeeded in driving out another. She now had no anxiety to spare for the approaching test of her acting ability. Her morale was at a very low ebb indeed when the coach rounded a bend on the narrow track to reveal before them a clearing in the forest on which stood an isolated, stone-built house. It was of a fair size, too big to be a forester's cottage, yet not large enough for a country squire's home. Emma guessed that it must be a hunting lodge which had stood there for several centuries. At sight of it, she fetched a deep sigh of relief.

The coachman took his vehicle through the open wooden gates, halting outside the door of the house. The groom beside him jumped down to help the young lady alight, and then plied the door knocker with energy. After a few moments, an elderly woman in black bombazine and a frilled mob cap came to the door.

"No call to knock it down," she said severely to the groom; then, turning to Emma, "Come you in, ma'am, and I'll show you to your room. The lad will bring your baggage on the instant."

Feeling reassured at once by the obviously respectable appearance of what she took to be the housekeeper, Emma stepped into the hall. It was not very large and somewhat gloomy, as the sun was on the back of the house and the surrounding forest cut off most of the light. She had little time to take stock of her surroundings, however, for the housekeeper led the way up a flight of uncarpeted wooden stairs and along a short passage until she reached a room near the end. She flung open the door, standing aside for Emma to enter.

"Here you are, ma'am. I dare say you'll want to wash the dust off after your journey, so I'll send one of the girls up with hot water. There are towels, as you see; and anything else you may need, pray ask, ma'am. And when you're ready, if you'll please to come downstairs again, there'll be a cold collation waiting in the dining parlour — I'll be in the hall myself to direct you."

A tap on the door announced the arrival of Emma's trunk and carpet bag. These were set down; the door closed and she was alone.

She looked about her. The bedchamber was far from luxurious, but it wore an air of comfort which had been totally lacking in the room she had occupied at Marton Hall. The four-poster bed felt soft to the touch and was covered with a brightly coloured patchwork quilt. There was a dressing table, wash stand and a low chair embroidered in petit point set before a fire which was laid ready for lighting. Against the window wall stood a small writing desk with bookshelves above it.

She opened a closet door to reveal ample hanging space for her small wardrobe, and began to unpack, humming softly to herself as she did so. Everything here appeared so normal, almost welcoming, that she felt reassured. Her fears on the journey now seemed absurd, the products of an over-active imagination.

The hot water arrived, and she washed and tidied herself, trying not to interfere too much with Antonia's arrangement of her hair. She told herself that she would soon become accustomed to doing it in the new style, and it certainly did make an improvement in her looks. In fact, as she studied herself finally in the mirror before leaving the bedchamber, she felt she had never looked as attractive for many years.

It gave her confidence which she was in need of when she descended the stairs and followed the housekeeper to a room on the ground floor. It had only one occupant, a lady in her late twenties dressed with quiet elegance in a pale blue and white striped lustring gown. She came forward to greet her visitor. Emma was momentarily too flustered to study the other woman closely but gained an impression of a pleasant countenance with a pair of intelligent brown eyes.

"Miss Maleverer, I believe?" Her voice was pleasant, too.

Emma inclined her head in answer, unable to force out the direct lie just yet.

"We are so glad you can be with us. Permit me to make myself known to you — I am Juliana Hythe. Won't you be seated at the table, and take some refreshment with me, ma'am?"

Emma sat down at a small table temptingly laid with a selection of cold meats and fruit. She had no appetite to speak of, but she allowed the lady to serve her with a small helping of food rather than risk giving offence at this early stage in their relationship. As the plate was handed to her, she noticed a wedding ring on Juliana Hythe's finger, and was glad of this clue as to how she should address her hostess.

While the meal was in progress, Mrs. Hythe chatted inconsequentially on general topics such as the weather, making no mention at all of the purpose of Emma's visit. At last, towards the end of the meal, Emma felt bound to introduce the subject herself.

"Are you my employer, ma'am?" she asked, diffidently.

Mrs. Hythe shook her head. "Oh, no — your services have been engaged by my brother, but he thought it might be more comfortable for you to meet me first. He will see you presently and explain everything." She paused, a little frown creasing her brows. "It is a somewhat — unusual — project. But," she added, brightening, "well within your professional capabilities, I am confident."

Emma, with good reason to doubt this, felt uneasy again. Fortunately, she was given no time to brood, however, for in a few minutes Mrs. Hythe rang for the meal to be cleared away and rose from her chair.

"Now if you are quite ready, Miss Maleverer, I will take you to my brother, and you can ask him anything you choose. Pray be good enough to follow me."

Emma obeyed with a pounding heart. Would she ever be able to sustain this monstrous deception? It needed only a small slip to make her betray herself, and then what would become of her? She might find herself turned out of doors for the second time in twenty-four hours. It was not an agreeable thought, and it helped to put her once more on her mettle. It was too late for misgivings — she must act for all she was worth.

The door to which Mrs. Hythe led her opened upon a book-lined room with windows looking out on a small lawn guarded by a neatly trimmed hedge. Beyond this was the forest, green and impenetrable. Emma's eyes had unconsciously gone to the windows at first, as though seeking escape; but now she saw that a gentleman had risen from his chair and was studying her closely.

"This is my brother, Rupert Wynford," said Mrs. Hythe. "Miss Maleverer." The gentleman bowed, and Emma responded with a curtsey. "Perhaps you would like me to leave you together, Rupert?"

"I think that will be best, Ju. Pray, be seated, Miss Maleverer."

He placed a chair for Emma, then walked across the room to open the door for his sister. Emma sat down, feeling surprisingly calm now that the ordeal had arrived. She studied Mr. Wynford with interest until he resumed his seat, when her curiosity became more guarded.

She judged that he could not be more than a year or so older than his sister. They were alike in colouring, with the same brown hair and eyes, but there the resemblance ended. The man's face was thinner, with a more prominent nose and a jutting jawline which suggested firmness, perhaps even ruthlessness. He was of a good height with broad shoulders, and his sporting attire was well cut.

So much she managed to take in before he was sitting opposite her, studying her in his turn.

He was silent for several minutes, then said abruptly, "You're younger than I had expected, ma'am."

Emma was a trifle disconcerted by this remark, but she decided to brazen it out. "I'm sorry, sir. It's a fault that time will remedy, however."

He laughed; and she gained the impression from the ready crinkles round his eyes that his face was no stranger to the exercise.

"True, ma'am. And in any case, it's of no consequence in this affair. Now, to business. I collect that you are a play actress of some years' experience; that you've been in the habit of playing minor parts with small touring companies; that you've been without employment for some time and that you have no personal ties?"

"That is correct," replied Emma, doing her best to look him straight in the eye.

"You must forgive me if I put this too bluntly," he continued, "but it's of the utmost importance that certain facts should be established. It's not then at all likely that your name — more important, your *face* — would be widely known to the public?"

"Not at all likely," agreed Emma, recollecting what Antonia had divulged of her career.

"And particularly not in Dorset? I believe you said as much at your interview in London, but we must be quite certain on this point."

Emma supposed that by "we" he must mean the rest of his family and wondered why her anonymity was so important to them. One might have supposed that they would prefer to employ the services of an actress who was tolerably well known. She was sure of her answer, though, both on Antonia's account and her own.

"No — I have never appeared anywhere in that county and have no acquaintance there."

"Ah, capital! That makes matters much simpler. And now just one further question, Miss Maleverer." He consulted a paper with some notes jotted on it, which he held loosely in one hand. "Tell me, is that your real name?"

Emma held her breath for a moment, thinking that she had been discovered as an impostor. He saw the change in her expression and frowned in a puzzled way.

"Come, ma'am," he said, encouragingly, "do not look so alarmed. I only mean to ask if Antonia Maleverer is a stage name."

She relaxed; of course, she ought to have realised that he could only mean that. She took a sudden decision. Here was a way out of one of her embarrassments, at any rate.

"Yes," she replied, a little breathlessly. "Yes, it is a stage name. My real name is Emma Harcourt."

"Harcourt? I knew a Harcourt once — but, of course, he could be no relation. And Emma —" he pondered the name for a moment — "Yes, Emma suits you a deal better than Antonia, and will be more suitable for our purposes, I think. Antonia Maleverer!" He smiled. "A trifle grandiloquent, but no doubt it is just the thing for your profession."

"Plain Emma Harcourt would not do at all, I assure you." She smiled in return, beginning to feel more at ease with him.

"Plain, ma'am? You do yourself less than justice."

He shot a keen look at her. To her dismay, she found herself blushing; that would never do. She could not imagine the real Antonia being so missish. Fortunately, he evidently thought it was deliberate.

"What, play-acting already?" he laughed. "That is one act you won't require in your new role — at least, not when you're playing opposite me, though you may be as modest as you choose with others. But come to think of it —" he went on, sobering quickly — "you're looking a trifle apprehensive, unless I mistake. There's no need — my sister will assure you that I'm quite harmless. It's true that this must be a somewhat unusual assignment for you. But once you're accustomed to the idea, I feel confident that you will give a splendid performance. Indeed —" he paused, a puzzled look coming over his face — "you are more of the type for the role than I had previously been led to believe."

Emma experienced a sinking feeling again. Everything that Mr. Wynford was saying pointed to a discrepancy between what he had learned of Antonia Maleverer from his London informant and the actual impression he was receiving of her now. It did not augur well for keeping up the deception, she thought. Unless — the idea came suddenly, bringing with it a flood of relief — unless she gave up any attempt to act as Antonia might, and instead allowed herself to behave naturally, at least in her off-stage relations with her employers. Of course, she would need at times to guard her tongue; but she had become so used at Marton Hall to suppressing all reference to her personal life, that this should not be difficult. What had Antonia said? That she had been acting the part of a governess; it was quite true.

She took a deep breath. "I don't quite understand you, Mr. Wynford. Certainly I have never before acted in private theatricals, but I believe it's not so very unusual for members of my profession to do so. I think perhaps it will be best if you tell me which play we are to perform and what part in it will be allocated to me. All I know so far is that my services have been engaged here for three months."

"Not here," he corrected quickly. "We shall be rehearsing here for less than a fortnight. The rest of your contract is for Dorset — that's why I had to know if you'd ever performed in the county before."

"I see," she said, slowly. There was a pause, then she suddenly burst out — "For the life of me, I cannot see why you should prefer an unknown actress!"

He gave her a long, serious look. "Not only unknown, but without friends in the county, or ties of any kind, and — shall we say? — not particularly successful. In short, someone who is desperate enough for money to agree to a somewhat — ah — unconventional assignment. And also —" he smiled cajolingly — "someone who is young enough, presentable enough and clever enough to bring it off successfully."

"I don't mind telling you, sir, that I do not at all care for the sound of this!" said Emma, roundly. "Kindly inform me about the play and my role in it!"

"As you wish. It's a real-life role, and yet a play," he replied, watching her intently. "You are to pretend to be my wife."

FIVE

Emma stared at him, wide-eyed, for a moment; then cast a desperate look at the door and edged forward in her chair, ready to escape.

"No, I am not mad," he assured her, gravely. "You have nothing to fear."

His manner was so sane that she could not really believe he was a lunatic. Yet what other explanation could there be? Perhaps she had not understood him properly.

"You mean — pretend to be your wife in real life — not just in a stage part?" she asked, breathlessly.

He nodded. "Exactly so."

"But — but it's absurd! Oh — are you perhaps in jest? Is this your notion of being amusing?"

He shook his head. "Never more serious, ma'am, I assure you."

"But — but —" she stammered. "*Why*? What in the world would be the purpose of such an — an imposture?"

"I fear I'm not at liberty to explain; but you may believe me when I say that there is a very serious purpose for this charade."

"That's all very well," said Emma, recovering her nerve, "but you cannot expect me to take the situation on trust. For all I know, I might be lending myself to some illicit enterprise."

He hesitated for a moment, "And if I give you my word that it isn't so?"

"Forgive me for speaking plainly, but what do I know of you, after all, sir? How can I tell whether or not your word is to be trusted?"

"You remind me of someone when you speak like that," he said, considering her with a frown. "Devil knows who — but you're something of a fire-eater, ma'am, ain't you?"

"Perhaps. I hope I can speak out when I think it necessary," replied Emma, with compressed lips.

"You puzzle me," he said, thoughtfully. "I understand that you are without employment and have no means of support other than what you can earn by your own efforts. I am prepared to offer you a not wholly contemptible sum for doing what you are trained to do, in more comfortable circumstances than must be usual in the acting profession. True, you will be required to sustain the role beyond what would be expected in the normal way, when your acting would be confined to the stage. But it was felt that the remuneration offered was sufficient to allow for this — a hundred guineas is surely not bad for three months' work! Don't you agree, ma'am?"

"A — a — *hundred* guineas?" gasped Emma.

He raised an eyebrow. "You don't think it enough, ma'am?"

"Enough!" she drew a deep breath, then burst out in an uncontrollable accession of frankness — "I could never hope to earn as much as that in the ordinary way in years put together!"

"No? I dare say not. Then perhaps that consideration may help to put your doubts at rest. I should mention that half of the sum will be payable in advance, and the remainder when your — ah — duties are completed." He looked at her questioningly. "I trust that this arrangement meets with your approval, ma'am?"

She made no answer for a moment. A hundred guineas would support her for a long period, certainly long enough to find herself a fresh post as a governess somewhere. If she accepted this mad offer, her future ought to be secure; should she refuse, on the other hand —

She shivered, then drew herself up, looking him squarely in the face.

"What exactly do you want me to do?"

"Ah, that's better!" he said, approvingly. "Briefly, then, I require you to pose as my wife. The act must be completely convincing, both to the servants and to neighbours. In order to make it so, I have brought you here to this isolated spot so that we may have the opportunity to rehearse together our parts before launching ourselves upon Dorset society as man and wife."

"But — completely convincing — does that mean — what I would say, is —"

She faltered, and felt the colour rising in her cheeks.

"I was informed that you are a spinster, ma'am," he said, in a business-like tone. "That is correct?"

She nodded.

"Then spare your blushes. I have no thought of exploiting the situation to force any unwelcome attentions on you, if that is what you fear. I shall be engaged in a venture which will demand my full attention, and I assure you I shall have neither the time nor the inclination for dalliance. But surely," he added, puzzled, "your experiences as an actress must have cured you of being at all missish?"

"You are not to think, sir, that all actresses are — are light women," replied Emma, using indignation to mask her feelings of embarrassment. "I'm aware that there is a popular notion to that effect but let me tell you it is quite mistaken!"

"I meant no offence, ma'am; merely that you must often have been called upon to speak words and enact scenes on the stage which might have raised a blush in a female leading a more sheltered kind of life. I'm quite prepared to believe that a lady of your profession may be as virtuous as the next woman. Pray pardon any unintentional offence on my part and let us waste no more time on that."

"Very well."

She inclined her head stiffly. His mouth twitched and she saw he was amused. He rose and crossed to a bureau, opening the top and taking out a paper written in a fine script.

"Here is — your part, I suppose we might call it," he said, handing her the paper. "It contains information which you would certainly be expected to possess as my wife — details of my past life and of our courtship and marriage. I need hardly say that the first is almost as fictitious as the second. I hope you will have the whole story off pat before we leave this house. We must also concoct between us some such fictional account of yourself. If you feel equal to it, we might attempt that later in the day. And now perhaps you will like to discuss with my sister the domestic arrangements for the house in Dorset — she has been supervising them. You will scarcely have been used to the ordering of a household, I suppose, but don't let that concern you unduly. Juliana tells me she has engaged a very good housekeeper for us."

"Mrs. Hythe will not be there herself?" asked Emma, uneasily.

"You'd best call her Juliana, since she's to be your sister-in-law," he suggested. "No, she has to return to her own family in Devon. She and her husband will remain here until we go to Dorset, however, to help us with our rehearsals."

"Then Mr. Hythe is here?"

"Yes, you will meet him this evening at dinner, and then our family circle will be complete. Well, I think that concludes our business for the present — unless there are any questions you'd like to put to me?"

Emma gave a shaky laugh. "Any questions! You present me with this — this outrageous scheme, and then calmly ask if I have any questions! Upon my word, sir, I can scarce be blamed for having the strongest doubts as to your sanity!"

"I understand your feelings," he said, in a gentler tone than he had used so far, "and, believe me, I sympathise in some measure. But if you can bring yourself to forget the unusual nature of the undertaking and think of it simply as one more part which you are called upon to play, I am confident we shall do very well. Indeed, we *must!*" he added, vigorously. "A great deal hangs upon this scheme — it's not just a playful hoax. No —" as she started to speak — "I can say no more on that head, so pray save your breath. Do the business for which you are trained and leave the rest to me."

Taking this as a dismissal, Emma started to rise; but he detained her with a gesture of his hand.

"One last thing — I collect that you are without relatives or friends. Would it be asking too much that you should inform *no one* of your present whereabouts?"

"No," she replied, readily enough. "There is no reason why I should, for there's no one to miss me."

He shot her a penetrating glance that might have held some compassion; but she could not be certain of this, as his expression changed the next moment to its former indifference.

"Capital — that's to say, nothing could better suit our purpose. I suppose I need hardly add that you must maintain the utmost secrecy about our plan? Confide in no one — trust no one. From now on, everyone here will treat you as my wife."

She left the room with her head in a whirl. Could the man be mad, after all? His manner was rational enough, it was true, but the scheme he had just proposed surely belonged to the realms of fantasy. Assuming that he was not deranged, what purpose could there be in it? Whom did he wish to deceive and to what end? Could she accept his word that there was no criminal purpose in the plan? She felt sure of nothing and wished she could see some other way out of her difficulty than taking part in this dubious project. But a hundred guineas! And the alternative was penury or perhaps worse, she reminded herself.

Juliana Hythe had been working on some embroidery but set it aside when Emma entered the parlour again.

"Pray sit down, ma'am," she said, smiling. "Have you and my brother reached an agreement?"

Emma nodded as she took a chair. "Yes, we have. But I must say, Mrs. Hythe, that I am completely at a loss to understand all this. Your brother is not —" she paused, unwilling to give offence, but determined to ask the question — "er — by any chance given to strange humours?"

"You mean you think he is out of his mind," stated Mrs. Hythe, simply. "And I suppose you can scarce be blamed for reaching that conclusion. No, you need have no fears whatever on that score — no one knows better what he is about than Rupert."

"Then I can only wish that he would tell *me* what he is about! Does he wish to practise this deception upon someone for his own advantage? He assured me that it's not just some foolish hoax — a wager, for instance. Gentlemen are, I know, often given to nonsense of that kind. I promise you, Mrs. Hythe, I can be discreet; and if you could only bring yourself to explain, it would make me so much easier in my mind."

Mrs. Hythe shook her head decisively. "I'm sorry for it, but that is quite out of the question. For one thing, I know very little of the matter; for another, if Rupert thinks you should know, he will tell you himself. In the meantime, you have only to think of it as a professional engagement, you know, and then you can be quite easy. You may safely trust Rupert in all things, I assure you."

"Very well," said Emma. "I mislike mysteries, but since you both say it must be so, I shall do my best to serve you. Mr. Wynford said I was to apply to you for details of the domestic arrangements in Dorset. Whereabouts in Dorset are we to go?"

"We have taken a house in a village a few miles from Weymouth. As you may know, the King goes there every year for his health, and the town is quite gay, so you will not lack for entertainment. But before I tell you about that, let us decide what I am to call you. Miss Maleverer won't do, since we are to play the part of sisters."

"Mr. Wynford and I agreed upon using my real name, not the stage one. It is Emma."

"Emma," Mrs. Hythe considered it. "Yes, I like that — it suits you, too. And you must call me Juliana, of course. I'll tell you all about myself, my husband and our children, so that you make no mistake there."

"I'm sorry that you won't be accompanying me to Dorset, ma'am — that is to say, Juliana." Emma corrected herself hurriedly. "It would be more comfortable for me to have another female in the household."

"Yes, I can quite see that." Juliana Hythe nodded sympathetically. "But you'll be mixing a good deal in the local society, you know, and as I said just now, Weymouth is a lively place at this season. You won't lack for female companionship, I promise you. The only thing is —" she hesitated, then went on — "you cannot be as open as perhaps you might wish in your friendships. You will need to keep a guard on your tongue and remember that you play a part."

"Your brother has already made that clear." Emma's tone was cool. "And I don't think I'm in any danger of forgetting the purpose for which I was engaged. But it was not the lack of female *companionship* that was troubling me. Indeed, I'm quite used to spending most of my time on my own."

"Then what —?" Juliana stared at her for a moment, then finished in an incredulous tone — "You surely can't be concerned over the proprieties? Oh, I mean no offence, believe me, but surely your years on the stage must have given you a less conventional outlook than that of more — sheltered — females? That was certainly what was supposed, in deciding to engage an actress for this service."

"You are answering much as your brother did. I can only repeat," said Emma, drily, "that my sense of propriety is as nice as it ever was."

"Oh, dear!" exclaimed Juliana, in dismay. "You aren't in the least as we imagined you would be! What is to be done, then? Do you wish to be quit of the affair?"

Emma made no reply. She was thinking, furiously. This was the point of no return, her last chance to turn back from a course that would certainly (if it ever became known) mean the loss of her reputation. But who was there now to care about her good name, since her father's death? And after all this was over, she could go and live somewhere miles away from the few places where she had been known — she could go to Cumberland, for instance, where her old schoolmistress lived. With a hundred guineas in her purse, such changes were possible.

Juliana broke into her thoughts at this point, unconsciously echoing them. "It's not as if anyone need ever know," she said, persuasively. "You're a stranger to the county, and so is my brother. People will accept you readily enough as man and wife — why should they not? Something is to be arranged for you afterwards; I don't know quite what, but it will be far enough away from Dorset, you may be sure."

Emma knew then that she was committed, for better or worse.

SIX

"This hamlet is called Poxwell," announced Wynford, breaking a long silence. "We shall come to the village of Osmington in another mile or so, and not long after that we turn off the main road for Poyntz Ferrers, our ultimate destination. You will not be sorry to get there, I dare say."

Emma agreed, rousing herself from the weary inertia of a long day's jostling in the carriage to gaze out of the windows with some semblance of interest at the passing scene. Poxwell was a cluster of thatched cottages and neat farm buildings lying among trees in the shelter of the surrounding Downs. It was soon passed, and then the road bent round to reveal a distant glimpse of the sea between the hills on their left; on the right, Emma's attention was caught by a white horse carved high on the hillside.

"A local landmark," said Wynford, following her gaze, "but not, I think, as old as some in other parts of the country. This is Osmington now — most of the village lies off the main road, but it's a pretty spot. I dare say we may ride over to see it, some time, if you should feel equal to the exercise."

This remark reminded Emma, even if she had been in any danger of forgetting it, that she was supposed to have come to Dorset in order to recover from an illness. But there was little likelihood of her forgetting her part in this bizarre play, because every single day of their stay in the New Forest had been spent in rehearsing their respective roles.

The confidence she now felt in her performance had not been gained without great effort. It had been comparatively simple to memorize the details of the manufactured biographies of Rupert Wynford and herself, and to answer the searching questions on these which were daily put to her by Wynford himself and by the Hythes. What had been much harder was to learn to behave with these strangers as if they were indeed her own relatives, and particularly to treat Rupert Wynford in a way that would convince the outside world that he was her husband. Several times she had seen his patience strained to breaking point when she had failed to achieve the right degree of familiarity in some of the test situations which were endlessly devised for her.

"It's well enough for you to address me as 'Mr. Wynford'," he said somewhat snappishly, on one occasion. "Wives frequently do so; but it would surely seem odd if a bride of some eighteen months or so did not slip in the occasional mild endearment — 'my love', 'my dear', that kind of thing. And do, pray, try to refrain from drawing away whenever I chance to touch your hand — for all the world as though I had red-hot fingers at least, if not the plague! Few men are such fools as to parade affection for their wives in public, even supposing they feel any such emotion," he added, cynically. "But a total avoidance of all contact must be noticed and would set tongues wagging. Our aim must be to present to the world a picture of an average married couple who, while well past the honeymoon stage, haven't yet had time to grow completely indifferent to each other."

"Such as ourselves," remarked Mr. Hythe, smiling at Juliana.

"No, not a bit like you two!" Wynford gave a crack of laughter. "Devil take it if I ever saw a more maudlin pair! No, Emma and I must try for something on a cooler plane, but *not* —" he fixed Emma with a look of command — "not so frigid as to suggest that all is not as it should be. Do I make myself clear?"

She nodded, swallowing back the resentment which she realised had no place in what was a business arrangement. Possibly a genuine actress might have been allowed the occasional show of temperament, but she did not intend to risk it. Instead, she tried to accept all criticism patiently, using it to make an improvement in her performance. Day by day, she learned to slough off the skin of Miss Harcourt, governess; even the intermediate stage of Antonia Maleverer playing a part was eventually forgotten. By the time they set off on their journey for Poyntz Ferrers, to all outward appearances she had become Rupert Wynford's wife.

Inwardly, there were many misgivings. With Juliana Hythe in the same house, she had felt a measure of protection which would now be lacking. Could she rely upon Mr. Wynford to keep his word about not trying to exploit the situation?

She had some reason to believe that she could. Although they had acted together the part of man and wife for close on a fortnight, she had so far never once detected in him the faintest flicker of interest in herself as a woman. Obviously, he regarded their arrangement as a strictly business one. She looked across at him now, sitting opposite her in the carriage, and their eyes met briefly. His held nothing but an abstracted indifference. She felt a faint stirring of resentment that she should be of so little consequence and told herself sharply not to be so foolish. The last thing she wanted was for him to take a personal interest in her.

"And here we are, my dear." Uttered in a cool tone, the endearment gave no surprise. It had been agreed that they were to keep up their play-acting as far as possible even when they were alone together, so that there was less chance of making a slip before company. "This is Poyntz Ferrers. Do you think you'll find the place tolerable for a few months?"

They had turned off the main road about half a mile back into a lane with a stream running beside it. The carriage slackened its pace and Emma had leisure to look about her on the right, hard by a small, grey stone church; on the left, farther along, the stream widened into a pond flanked by willows. A small footbridge across this gave access to a row of picturesque thatched cottages on the other side. Behind the village rose the green hill slopes, touched with that evening light which gives a golden lustre to the countryside.

"It's beautiful," she said, with a ready response to the charm of the scene.

"Yes, indeed it is," agreed Wynford, as the carriage turned into a gateway on the right, just beyond the bridge. "You may perhaps find it a trifle rural for your taste, but Weymouth is close at hand, and I understand the local gentry are of a friendly disposition."

They passed along a winding drive bordered by chestnuts to the house itself, a small Tudor manor of stone mellowed by age, with mullioned windows reflecting the rays of the declining sun. A high wall encircled the grounds, which did not appear extensive. This, together with the sheltering hills rising behind, gave the place an air of refuge; or so Emma thought on that first view of it. Afterwards, she was to wonder how she could have been so mistaken.

The interior of Poyntz Manor pleased her. Little had been done to modernise it; oak beams and panelling had been left in their original state, and the low ceilings were of intricately decorated plaster. Everything was well cared for, and more to Emma's own taste than the more usual modern classical interiors, which could sometimes give a cold air to a house. Besides, it reminded her of the cottage where she had spent some months with her father during his last furlough.

She was received by the housekeeper, Mrs. Hinton, a pleasant woman in early middle age, whose capable looks bore out Juliana Hythe's assurance that domestic affairs could safely be left in her hands. She lost no time in conducting Emma up a wide staircase to a bedchamber on the first floor.

"Shall I send your maid up now, ma'am?" she asked.

Emma untied her bonnet and laid it on the bed. "Not immediately, thank you, Mrs. Hinton. What time have you arranged for dinner?"

"That depends on you, of course, ma'am, but Cook and I were thinking that seven o'clock might suit — not that it couldn't be put forward or back, should you so wish," replied the housekeeper, secure in the knowledge that Cook had been warned of this contingency. It was as well to go carefully with Cook, a lady with an artistic temperament to match her undoubted culinary talent.

Emma consulted her watch, a valued present from her father. "That's to say in an hour's time. It will do very well. And if you could ask Matilda to come to me in about twenty minutes, I'd be grateful."

The housekeeper curtseyed and withdrew. Emma, glad to be on her feet for a while after so many hours of sitting in the coach, walked about the room examining everything. There was the same care for her comfort here that she had found in the other house, but the furnishings of this room were on a more luxurious scale. The fourposter bed of elaborately carved mahogany had blue velvet curtains and a bedspread of blue brocade; the carpet was so thick that her feet sank soundlessly into it. An array of silver-backed brushes and glass cosmetic bottles were laid out on the dressing-table, and the washing stand held a dainty flower-patterned toilet set. She was pleased to see an empty glass-fronted bookcase and bureau standing against the window wall; here was a place for her own books.

She noticed that there were two doors in the room, apart from the entrance door. She opened one to reveal a small powder closet; then she tried the other, which was set in the wall against which the bed-head rested. To her surprise, this gave on to another bedchamber similar in size to her own. She stepped over the threshold to look around, and soon made the discovery that this was a gentleman's room. She retreated hastily, blushing in spite of herself, and firmly closed the door.

And then it dawned on her with dismay that this must be the room which Rupert Wynford was to occupy. They had been put in adjoining bedchambers at the house in the New Forest. It was not so very unusual in genteel society for husband and wife to occupy separate rooms; but just in case the arrangement should occasion remark from the servants, Juliana Hythe had let it be known that Emma was recovering from an illness and frequently slept badly.

Emma had not liked occupying a room next door to Wynford's, but she realised it was necessary to their deception, and it had not interfered in any way with her privacy. But a communicating door between their bedchambers was altogether another matter!

She conquered her dismay with an effort. After all, a door could be locked. There was certainly a lock on the door, but no key in it. Perhaps it was on the other side. She pulled the door open again, but no — there was no key on that side, either. A bolt — there must be a bolt on it somewhere, she told herself and frantically searched both sides of the door for one, but without success.

She paused then, her hands slightly clammy from agitation. Where could the missing key be? Had it perhaps fallen out of the lock when she had first tugged at the door? It would have made no sound on the soft carpet — yes, that would be it. She dropped to her knees and passed her hands over the thick pile of the carpet, first on her own side of the door, then on the other. After a while, she shook her head and rose again, dusting down her gown with fingers that trembled. What should she do now? There was a lock on the door, so there must be a key to it somewhere, and the likelihood was that it would be somewhere in this room. She looked about her, debating where to make a start on her search.

Her eye fell on the entrance door to the room, and she gave a little exclamation of relief. Of course! There was a key in that lock, and most likely it would also fit the lock of the communicating door. She rushed across the room to seize the key and make the attempt. She soon realised it was impossible; this was not the key she sought. Thrusting it back impatiently into its own keyhole, she began a frantic search of the room.

It did not take long, because there were as yet no personal belongings in the drawers and cupboards. She inspected them all, then turned her attention to trinket boxes and any other small receptacles which might be supposed to conceal a key. At length she threw up her hands in a gesture of disgust, acknowledging defeat. The wretched key was nowhere in this room, that much was certain. Was it perhaps to be found in the adjoining one?

She paused beside the door, half minded to go in and look. But her maid Matilda would be coming up with her luggage at any moment; besides, Mr. Wynford himself might arrive and find her in his room. The thought brought some colour to her cheek. What else could be done? The obvious course of asking the housekeeper for the key was one she dare not take. Mrs. Hinton might well wonder why her mistress wished to lock the door of her bedchamber against her husband. It was the kind of thing which Mr. Wynford had particularly warned Emma against. There was nothing else for it, she thought with a fatalistic shrug; she must take the first opportunity to tell him about the missing key and ask him to make a search for it in his own room. If it still could not be found, no doubt he would think of some way of obtaining another. He struck her as being a man of infinite resource.

Matilda's arrival put an end to these thoughts for the time being. Mrs. Hythe had brought Matilda with her to the house in the New Forest so that the girl might train as Emma's personal maid and later accompany her new mistress to Dorset. Matilda was no fashionable lady's maid, but a country girl who had started in service in Mrs. Hythe's own household a year or so previously. She had deft hands and a good eye for colour, but was of a placid, incurious disposition, unlikely to gossip about her employers with the other servants. These attributes had seemed to Mrs. Hythe to make her the ideal choice for the post. Emma, who had never before had a maid to wait upon her, thought at first that she might find it tiresome; but she had been grateful for Matilda's help with the new hair style devised for her by Antonia Maleverer, and gradually became accustomed to the girl's unobtrusive assistance in other ways.

It was as well that Matilda did not have a lively, inquiring mind, or she might have wondered at the inadequacy of her mistress's wardrobe. She bustled about now, pouring out warm, scented water into one of the flower-patterned basins for Emma to wash, and then unpacking the luggage which had been brought up by a footman.

At Emma's instructions, she laid out one of the few evening gowns contained in the trunk, inspecting it doubtfully.

"'Twould be better for pressing, ma'am," she said diffidently.

Emma glanced at the gown and shook her head. "There isn't time, Matilda. Besides, it will do for this evening — there'll only be Mr. Wynford and myself dining alone."

The girl continued with the unpacking, leaving off after a while to help Emma into the gown, and then to arrange her hair. After this was done, Emma rose to inspect herself in the long mirror standing beside the dressing table. She took a long look, then sighed.

Her gown was of plain white cambric with a crossover neck modestly filled in by a white muslin tucker and finished at the waist with a pale blue sash. She possessed few pieces of jewellery but had looked out a pair of pearl earrings given to her long ago by her father. In spite of the new hair style, the whole effect, she decided, was demure to the point of dullness. Still, what did it matter? She was only dining with her employer — no, her husband. She must not forget that for a moment.

One topic was uppermost in her mind as she joined him in the oak-panelled dining parlour, but it could not be broached until the servants had left them. Instead, they shared a trivial conversation about the room and its furnishings. When the meal was finished, she rose from the table to leave him with the wine.

"I shan't be long before I join you," he said, as he rang the bell for a footman, "but only for a short while, I fear, as I have to go out presently. There is something I'd like to say to you first, though."

Her spirits sank a little on hearing this: and she could only hope that whatever he had to say would not take up so much time that there would be none left for her to mention the key.

There had been no opportunity yet for her to see all over the house, and so far she had not entered the drawing room. She was struck at once by its charm. Here the panelling had been painted white as a concession to modern taste, but it was hung with tapestries. A warm red carpet covered the floor and comfortable chintz-covered wing chairs were set either side of the wide, stone fireplace, in which a small fire burned, for late summer nights could be cool. An old-fashioned harpsichord stood against one wall, and Emma wondered idly who had last played it.

She sat down in one of the armchairs, but although it was comfortable; she could not relax. She kept watching the door for Wynford to appear. He did so barely ten minutes later, but it seemed an age to Emma. He came in briskly, shutting the door behind him, and stood surveying her for a moment in silence.

"Stand up, Emma," he commanded suddenly.

She obeyed, wondering what was to follow. He looked her over critically, from head to foot, then shook his head in a dissatisfied way.

"No, it won't do."

"What won't do? What do you mean?" she asked, puzzled.

"Juliana was right," he said, with an air of decision. "You must have some new clothes. That gown's the best of your evening attire, and that's not to say much. Oh, I'm not blaming you," he added quickly, seeing an uncomfortable flush in her cheeks. "There's been no money to spare — I realise that. But we shall shortly be mixing in local society, and my wife must be as well dressed as any other female. Juliana supplied me with the name of a very good mantua maker and milliner in Weymouth — we'll pay her a visit tomorrow, I think. I must admit it's not much in my line — it's women's work, and I'd gladly leave you to it, could I rely upon you to be extravagant enough! I have the oddest notion you'd be positively miserly — an unusual complaint for a husband to make, ain't it?"

"I — it is all rather awkward," she stammered.

"Not a bit," he said, bracingly, but in a lower tone. "You have only to remember that we must keep up appearances and think of it as stage costume. Juliana supplied me with a list of your probable requirements — I have it about me somewhere." He drew a leather notecase from his pocket and extracted a sheet of paper from it. "Here it is," he said, handing her the paper. "You might care to glance through that later on and add anything else you may think necessary."

"Heavens!" exclaimed Emma, after a quick look at the list. "I am more likely to cross off several items, I should think."

"No, that you mustn't do." His tone was firm. "I rely completely on my sister's judgement in all matters of female attire. Besides, there are no end of fashionable females in Weymouth during this season, and you must be as well dressed as any. Don't argue, but do as I bid you, like a good girl. It will give you something to occupy you during the rest of the evening, while I am out. Pray forgive me — I must go now."

"Oh, but I must speak to you for a moment," said Emma, hurriedly. "There is something that cannot wait — but I need not detain you for more than a few minutes."

"What is it?" he asked, surprised. "There's nothing wrong, I trust?"

"Not precisely." She found it difficult to begin on what she had to say and was not helped by seeing him glance surreptitiously at the clock. "It's just that — there's a communicating door between our bedchambers," she blurted out, in desperation, "and no means of securing it that I can see. I wonder if —"

To her dismay, he laughed. "Lud, is that all that's troubling you?"

"I should have thought it was sufficient," she answered, with cold dignity.

"Good God, Emma, how can you be so absurd?" he asked impatiently. "What do you expect me to do — ask the housekeeper for a key? That would put the cat among the pigeons, for sure!"

"No, I realise we cannot do that. But I thought perhaps you might look for it in your room — I've already searched mine without success."

"Devil take it!" he exclaimed, in a sudden spurt of anger. "You're as full of scruples as any Bath miss! One would have supposed your years on the stage might have a trifle blunted such tender susceptibilities! However, I will look for it later, but if I don't find it, you must contrive to manage without." He paused, and added in cooler, ironical tones — "But if you could possibly rid yourself of the persuasion that I shall attempt to turn our make-believe marriage into a real one, we should do a deal better, ma'am."

She coloured, her eyes snapping at him. "I think you're the most odious man I've ever met!"

To her surprise, he laughed good-humouredly. "Why, to be sure I am! Lud, what a jest for us to be quarrelling like any old married couple! I congratulate you, Emma — you give a superb performance. You must admit that in this mood you'd try the patience of a saint!"

She recovered her poise with an effort. "Thank you," she replied, with a little bow. "But since you're no saint, I can hardly be said to have the means of judging."

"One round each, I think." He chuckled appreciatively. "A pity to put an end to this most entertaining conversation, but I must go. Don't wait up for me — I shall be late. Au revoir, sweet fire-eater."

He kissed the tips of his fingers to her mockingly as he went from the room.

SEVEN

After he left her, Rupert Wynford went upstairs to his room and rang for his valet, who appeared promptly. Considering his profession, Burton was a surprisingly muscular young man, a few inches taller than his employer and sufficiently good looking for his arrival to have caused quite a stir among the female staff. They were a trifle overawed, however, by the superior accent which no doubt he had acquired through years of service as a gentleman's gentleman.

Wynford was hastily throwing off his evening dress. "Find me my riding things, there's a good chap," he said. "Wouldn't bother you, but I'm on the late side — meeting Abney in Weymouth."

Burton opened a closet door, producing a pair of buckskin breeches and an olive-green coat which he laid over a chair. He then took out a pair of well-polished boots and inspected them critically.

"Delayed somewhat by madam," explained Wynford, as he put on his breeches. "Some maggot in her head about a key — you might have a look round, see if it's lying about anywhere here — key to that door."

He jerked his head towards the communicating door. Burton glanced at it and chuckled.

"Don't trust you, eh, Rupert? Not without reason, if she knew all, must say."

"Devil a bit of it!" grunted his master, fastening the last button and reaching for his coat. "Here, give me a hand with this, will you? Defy the most hardened libertine to take advantage of such a proper miss — anyone'd think she'd been reared in the strictest of young ladies' seminaries, instead of leading the kind of life she must have had. Not saying that I mightn't have seized my chance, had she been more what I expected, but it's all in the luck of the game, what? And anyway, don't do to mix business with pleasure."

Burton agreed and began to draw on Wynford's boots.

"No, devil take it, I can manage that myself," protested the other. "Tell you what, she's a better actress than I hoped for, and fits the part of a respectable wife to perfection. Well, see what you can do about a key for that door, and keep an eye on things generally."

"Don't think I should come with you?" asked the valet, doubtfully.

"Good God, no! The fewer of us the better — besides it won't do to be seen about together, now, will it? I'm off, then — back soon after midnight, I hope. Hang about to let me in but see to it that the rest of the staff are all abed. I expect they will be."

He left the house unobtrusively, and made his way to the stables, where everything was in darkness. Without troubling to rouse any of the stable hands, he saddled and bridled his own bay horse by the light of a small dark lantern which he carried with him. Accustomed to his master's habits, the animal submitted quietly while Wynford fastened holsters to the saddle and checked the pistols which he thrust into these. This done, he mounted and began to ride across the stableyard.

The inevitable clatter of hoofs on the cobblestones roused one of the hands, who flung open a window, demanding to know who was there. Wynford's voice reassured him, however, and the window closed again.

The night was moonless, so Wynford had to pick his way carefully until he joined the turnpike road. He was not too familiar with the locality, although he had spent several days reconnoitring when Poyntz Manor had first been selected for his purpose. It was pleasant to feel the night air on his face, but he never relaxed completely for a second. Always he kept a sharp eye out for other travellers abroad, though there were few vehicles on the road, and the only pedestrian he saw was a labourer turning into a hedge tavern in search of refreshment.

It was not long before he reached the outskirts of Weymouth. Here he made a wide detour to avoid the fashionable streets of the town, coming out on the other side of the harbour beyond Newton's Cove. At this point, he took a cliff path for about half a mile, then reined in his horse and dismounted,, tethering the animal in the cover of a bush.

He took one of the pistols from its holster and thrust it into a thick leather belt which he had fastened about his waist. Then, unhooking the dark lantern from the saddle, he proceeded on foot along a rough track which wound down the cliff to the beach. Beside him was the sea, a dark mass sounding a gentle, melancholy plaint in the otherwise silent night. The sky above was of a lighter colour against which, when his eyes became accustomed, the ragged outlines of a ruined castle took shape.

He paused, adjusting the lantern to allow a glimmer of light to guide his footsteps as he cautiously climbed up among rocks and fallen masonry until he came to that part of the ruin which was still standing.

He paused then, within the shadow of a sheltering wall, and called softly once with the hoot of an owl.

A flutter of wings from above showed that he had momentarily disturbed a nesting bird, but there was no other sound.

He waited a while, then uttered the call a second time. A rustle sounded in the undergrowth behind him. He turned swiftly, pushing the shutter across his lantern with his left hand, pistol poised ready in his right. But it was only some marauding animal; in the second before the light was doused he had glimpsed the outline of its body streaking into the brambles.

For some time longer he waited, then gave the call again. Still no answer came. He eased the lantern's shutter to give some light, and slowly began a tour of the ruined castle. He came to a flight of broken steps; descending part of the way, he crouched down and increased the light so that its rays penetrated the gloomy hole beneath the staircase.

And then he saw the body.

After Wynford's departure, Emma took herself to task for making a fuss over the missing key. It was foolish of her to keep surprising him with her concern for the proprieties. What she kept forgetting — and certainly dare not forget — was that Mr. Wynford and his family believed her to be an actress. That being so, they might reasonably expect her to take a more relaxed view of the enforced intimacy of the situation. Members of a company on tour no doubt often had to make do with inadequate accommodation and live at closer quarters than strict propriety would dictate. Juliana Hythe had said that it was for reasons such as this that a professional actress had been decided upon.

She must be more careful not to arouse any suspicion that she was other than they thought her. No matter what happened, she resolved firmly, there must be no more maidenly shrinkings. Her reputation, in any case, was already irretrievably lost in the eyes of the world. That did not signify, for it could affect no one but herself, even if the masquerade ever became known. Who was there to care about the good name of an indigent governess?

She acknowledged to herself that, oddly enough, she had no real fears for her virtue; almost from the first, she had accepted his assurance that he had no wish to exploit the situation. It was just as she had thought in the coach coming here — he was scarcely aware of her as a woman. She was nothing but a stage property, thought Emma indignantly. Even as this crossed her mind, she smiled ruefully at her indignation. What else could she expect, or want?

She broke away from these reflections to wonder where he had gone. Some gentlemen's club in Weymouth, perhaps. He must have some acquaintance in the neighbourhood, as he had spoken of entertaining and being entertained; yet surely not very close acquaintances, or they would know that he was not really a married man. But did *she* know that? The question brought her up with a jerk. He might well have a wife somewhere whom his acquaintance in Dorset knew of but had never met.

The thought disturbed her, and to escape it she picked up the list which he had left with her. She was startled by the number of items it contained. *Three dozen* pairs of stockings — was that really necessary? But why quibble over stockings, when there were day gowns, evening gowns, riding habits, pelisses, spencers, shawls, shoes, gloves and goodness knows what besides? Surely she could never wear half of it in three months? It would cost a fortune, too, and he was to pay for it. Think of it as stage costume, he had said. Very well, she would, but not one single item would go with her when she quitted this post. On that she was determined.

She put the list away in her reticule and settled down to read a book. But she was tired from the day's journey and her eyelids kept drooping, so at last she decided to go early to bed. After her hair was done and Matilda dismissed, she settled thankfully between the sheets and was soon fast asleep.

She did not know what disturbed her, but suddenly she was wide awake, listening. She gradually became conscious of a murmur of voices from the adjoining room and the muffled sound of footsteps pacing up and down. She relaxed with a sigh. Evidently Mr. Wynford had returned and was talking to his valet, Burton. The man had been with them in the New Forest, and had struck Emma as unusually genteel, even for a personal manservant.

She turned over, preparing to settle off to sleep again; but just then a snatch of conversation came quite clearly to her ears.

"It was Abney. Dead as mutton — been lying in the castle ruins for days, I'd say. Not many people likely to go there, of course, which makes it a good spot for dumping a body."

The voice seemed to come through the communicating door. She sat up abruptly, turning her head towards it, then realised with a shock that it was not quite shut. A glimmer of light showed round the edge.

Quietly she eased herself out of bed and moved stealthily towards the door, her bare feet making no sound on the thick pile of the carpet. She was groping cautiously for the handle so that she might close the door without drawing attention to herself, when the next words, in the valet's voice, made her pause.

"Anything on him of value?"

She had not intended to eavesdrop, but curiosity got the better of her.

"Not a thing — cleaned out completely." This time it was Wynford speaking. "Even the ring had gone."

"Then you'd best look out for yourself, Rupert. No saying they didn't pick up something to lead to you — it's a dangerous game."

"No, there wouldn't be anything — you know the rules. Besides, the girl makes excellent cover for me. A man on his own may be marked, but what more normal than a man and his wife staying in Weymouth at this season? But the devil's in it that we've lost all we hoped to gain from Abney, as they got to him first. So we're no nearer —" The voice trailed away to an indistinct murmur. Evidently the two men had moved to another part of the room, too far away for her to hear.

Too terrified now to risk discovery, by attempting to close the door, Emma crept back to bed, pulling the covers close about her. She was shivering, although the room was warm enough.

What could the conversation mean? She was the girl who made excellent cover for Wynford, of course — but cover for what? It was a question she had asked him in the beginning without obtaining an answer and had posed to herself many times since. What she had just overheard suggested that his purpose in the deception was a sinister one. A man had been found dead. Murdered — by whom? And it sounded as though Wynford had intended to rob the unfortunate victim, or else by some means to persuade him to part with something valuable that had been in his possession. If Wynford had not found the man already dead, had he himself intended —

She shivered again, seeing Wynford for the first time as a figure of menace. Burton must also be involved in his employer's machinations, for it seemed he knew Wynford's secrets, even the closely guarded one of the marriage masquerade. She recalled, too, that he had called Wynford familiarly by his first name. Perhaps Burton was no more a valet than she was an actress; perhaps they were all involved in some monstrous game of make-believe. A dangerous game, Burton had said. But to what purpose? Where would it all end?

The next moment, she almost fainted from shock.

The communicating door was thrust open a foot or so, and in the faint light which came through the gap she could see a head silhouetted, peering into her room.

"Emma!" It was Rupert Wynford's voice, speaking in a whisper. "Emma, are you awake?"

It would be too dangerous to answer. Her heart was pounding and every nerve in her body quivered, but she forced herself to be still and feign sleep. Eyes tightly closed, hardly daring to breathe, she waited motionless for the dreaded moment when he would come over to the bed to look down at her.

But it never came. After what seemed like a lifetime of suspense, she heard the door shutting softly. It was some time before she dared to raise her head to look, but when she at last plucked up courage, she could no longer see the light round the door's edge. Evidently, one of the men had discovered that it was not quite shut, and Wynford had thought it wise to make sure that she could not possibly have overheard any of their conversation. Well, he had failed in that, at any rate, she thought grimly.

She was safe enough now, but her nerves were too frayed for sleep. She lay tossing and turning, considering what action to take. Her first thought was to leave as soon as it was light, before the servants were astir. She was not without money now; she had fifty guineas which Wynford had insisted on paying her in advance for her services. It was a fortune to her.

But no, she could not take all of it; it had not yet been earned. She would take what she was entitled to, and not a penny more, even though the money had most likely been stolen by him in the first place. Her weary brain struggled reluctantly with the mathematical calculation involved, and at last produced the answer that she would be entitled to about fifteen pounds. That had been a whole year's salary at Marton Hall, but their board and lodging had been included. How long would it last with these items to be paid for? She had little enough to add to it from her own slender savings.

The tears pressed at her tired eyelids, but she screwed them up defiantly. Freedom of action was always limited in the end by economic necessity. But was it this consideration alone which was urging her to stay in spite of everything? Perhaps she was too much her father's daughter not to see an enterprise through to its conclusion. Perhaps curiosity was stronger than apprehension; she wanted to know more about Rupert Wynford, to solve the mystery of the masquerade in which he had involved her.

She flung aside the tumbled covers of her bed and trod softly across the floor to her window. The pink tints of dawn were streaking across the sky; now was the time to go.

But she was not going. Oddly reassured, she crept back to bed, and was soon in a deep slumber.

EIGHT

Wynford's conduct at the breakfast table did nothing to suggest that he had spent the previous night in some form of villainy. He greeted her animatedly and kept up a cheerful flow of trivial conversation throughout the meal. After it was over, he asked her when she could be ready to accompany him into Weymouth.

"To Weymouth?" She was puzzled at first.

"Yes — to the gown shop I told you of — Madame Whatsitsname — surely you recall?"

He frowned at her warningly as he spoke, in case she should say something indiscreet in front of the servant who was clearing the table. But he need not have worried, as she showed him by her reply.

"Oh, to be sure! I am looking forward to it prodigiously! But are you sure you will like to come, my love? It will be tedious work for you, I fear."

He laughed. "That I expect, but I can't be such a brute as to leave my wife to face unattended the hazards of a strange town. Besides, I trust our errand will soon be done so that we can enjoy a stroll along the Esplanade. Now how soon can you be finished with your household duties? Will eleven o'clock suit you?"

She agreed readily to this and then went to seek out Mrs. Hinton, who took her on the tour of inspection for which she had been too tired yesterday evening. Their unexpected intrusion into the kitchen caused a scullery maid to become so jittery that she dropped a saucepan she was carrying. Fortunately, it was empty, so no harm was done beyond a sound scolding from Cook for the offender. Emma then inspected and approved the day's menus, apart from the inclusion of a blackcurrant pudding, which she vetoed firmly because Mr. Wynford disliked blackcurrants. Secretly, she was quite proud of having learnt her part well enough to remember this small fact.

Punctually, at eleven, he was helping her into the carriage. She wore Antonia's gown with the pink flowers embroidered on it, and a simple straw bonnet which she had trimmed with matching ribbons during their stay in the New Forest. He looked at her approvingly as they seated themselves and the carriage moved away.

"I like that best of all your gowns," he remarked. "All the rest are so sober! But I do believe —" he lowered his voice, though there was no danger of their being overheard at present — "you're rather a sober young lady. Or perhaps you consider that is the character best suited to the part of my wife?"

Emma scarcely knew what to say but smiled as though she agreed.

"Well, you're out in that," he continued. "I should never marry a woman who was too much of a sobersides, or she would drive me to drink! Neither," he added, reflectively, "would I want one of these hen-witted, giggling girls who are unable to take part in so much as ten minutes' rational conversation. But your interpretation will do well enough — indeed, splendidly — if you will but give it a lighter touch, now and then. You can be a little more yourself, you know, now that we've had some practice in our roles. You're every inch a well-bred female, but pray allow yourself to relax a trifle now and then."

"So you are not married?" she ventured to ask.

"Lud, no! Did you think I might be?"

"You might be anything, for all I know," replied Emma, with forced lightness.

"Very true; but that is one folly that so far I've escaped."

"You consider marriage foolish?"

"For most, probably — for me, certainly."

"Why more so for you?" She had not meant to let her curiosity get the better of her, but the opportunity to discover something about his personal life could not be resisted. "You think perhaps that you are temperamentally unsuited to it?"

He pursed his lips consideringly. "Not that, precisely. I dare say I could settle down quite comfortably with the right kind of woman. But my way of life at present precludes it."

Much as she wanted to question him further, she knew that on this subject it was useless. She had tried before and been very thoroughly snubbed for her pains. So she sat quietly for some time until the coach slowed up and pulled over into the side of the road in order to let two approaching waggons pass. They were piled high with logs, brushwood and tar barrels.

"It appears that someone means to start a prodigious blaze," she commented, by way of making conversation again.

"Firing for the beacons," he explained, briefly.

"Beacons?"

"Yes, as a warning in case of invasion. I dare say you may not have thought much on such matters where you come from, but down here on the Dorset coast, they are very much alive to the danger, I assure you. All kinds of elaborate plans have been made to meet the contingency, including the removal of women and children to safe places farther inland. When you have some acquaintance in the area, you'll most likely find the topic cropping up fairly frequently in the conversation."

She was silent for a moment. "You are quite right," she said, at last, "I hadn't seriously considered the possibility of a French invasion before. It's not an agreeable thought. Do you really suppose they may land, sir?"

"At this very moment," he said, grimly, "there is an army of a hundred thousand fine, well-trained men stationed at Boulogne — the Iron Coast, they call it. And a fleet of easily beached boats is ready and waiting to convey these troops across the Channel. Given the right conditions — a calm sea and the dark of the moon — and they will certainly attempt it."

She shivered at his tone. "But the Fleet — Lord Nelson —"

"It's impossible for the Fleet to stand close in shore near the French ports at all times and in all weathers. The most competent blockade can be evaded, given strategy and patience — and I think Bonaparte does not lack either requisite."

She stared at him in silence for a moment. "You speak almost as though," she said, slowly, "you not only expected, but even welcomed a landing on our shores."

He laughed shortly. "Do I? But I must not weary you with such tedious stuff! Here we are in Weymouth now, and you'll soon have something more agreeable to think of."

Madame Tiffany, milliner and mantua-maker, occupied an elegant bow-windowed premises in one of the fashionable streets quite close to the harbour. Wynford directed the coachman to wait, then helping Emma to alight, paused to look in the window for a moment before entering the shop. It was by no means crammed with goods. A few hat-stands were arranged against a background of skilfully swathed, lustrous dark red satin; on these perched the most mouth-watering specimens of ladies' headgear.

"Hm!" said Wynford, smiling down at his companion. "Such restraint in window dressing is usually accompanied, in my experience, by extreme prodigality in prices."

"And your experience of ladies' gown shops is no doubt extensive." She smiled in return.

He threw up his hands in mock dismay. "Ah, there you have me, my dear! But I am determined not to betray myself."

They went into the shop laughing quietly together, a fact which did not escape the comprehensive appraisement of Madame Tiffany, who came forward herself to receive them, waving back the assistant who had started to do this. The proprietress was a tall, slender woman with dark hair dressed in a classical top-knot, and a thin face in which a beaky nose was the most prominent feature. She had an arrogant expression and Emma disliked her on sight, but a very little time in her company was sufficient to show that she understood her business to perfection.

Wynford took charge of the proceedings with smooth assurance, making their wants known with a slightly uxorious air which Emma found irritating but which Madame Tiffany appeared to welcome, perhaps as a promise of open-handed dealing. She invited them to sit down on an elegant gilt sofa with a striped satin covering and ran a shrewd eye over Emma's proportions.

"Madame is fortunate," she said, with a cold smile, "in having a figure suited to the present mode. And since madam is not quite jeune fille, I venture to think we need not scruple to vary the fashionable white with soft shades of pink, blue or yellow — most becoming with ladies of madam's colouring. To give you some notion of styles, permit me to show you one or two gowns which I have made up ready for display."

She signalled to the assistant, who nodded and glided from the room. In a few moments, a willowy female appeared from the region beyond the showroom, attired in a graceful walking dress of blue cambric with a "waistcoat" bosom, and a flounce round the hem.

"Now that," remarked Rupert Wynford, judicially, "would become you extremely, my love."

"I am pleased that you should be of my opinion, Mr. Wynford," said Madame Tiffany. "Perhaps we may have the favour of making up this gown for your wife? There are, however, one or two others I would like you to see before arriving at a decision."

"By all means." Wynford settled more comfortably on the sofa with an expansive smile. "We will see them all — what do you say, Emma?"

Once again his expression irritated her, but she could not allow this to show. She returned his smile in what she hoped was a suitably coy manner, and murmured agreement.

After that, garments were paraded in rapid succession — walking dresses, day dresses, riding habits, ball gowns, pelisses — until Emma felt as if she were in a living dream. Never had she imagined setting eyes on so many fashionable and expensive clothes, much less being able to possess them. Everything was pressed upon her by her supposed husband, without any possibility of a refusal on her part. What genuine wife would be likely to refuse the chance of such a wardrobe?

When at last they had seen everything and their magnificent order had been given, Madame Tiffany requested Emma's attendance for a few moments in a private room at the back of the premises for the purpose of taking her measurements.

"I have a tolerable notion of what they will be, madam, but it's as well to make sure. If you will have the goodness to go with my assistant, your husband and I can discuss one or two matters in your absence."

As nothing so vulgar as price had so far been mentioned, Emma realised quite well what the matters under discussion would be. The bill for all these clothes would be a heavy one; Wynford must be a wealthy man. As she followed the assistant from the showroom, she reflected that this was quite likely, in view of the suspicions she entertained about him.

They went along a short passage and halted before a curtained alcove. The girl swept the curtain quickly aside, then started back, apologising in some confusion. The compartment was already occupied by another assistant who was just fastening a gown of pale green satin for a young lady with red-gold hair and a round, dimpled face.

The young lady looked startled at first, then began to laugh. "No, pray don't go away!" she exclaimed. "We have quite done, have we not, Berenice? If you wish to come in, I am going directly."

She had such an easy, friendly manner that Emma found herself smiling as she apologised for the intrusion.

"Not at all," replied the other, drawing on the gloves which had been handed to her by the girl called Berenice. "I am for ever bursting into places myself, so I'm the last to take offence. It makes life more interesting, don't you agree, ma'am? But I don't recollect seeing you here before — are you a new client of Madame Tiffany's? There! Now you'll think me impertinent for asking! But my tongue runs away with me, you know!"

She did speak very rapidly, and with a childlike enthusiasm which Emma found difficult to resist. In any case, there seemed no harm in admitting that this was her first visit to the gown shop.

"Oh, then perhaps you have taken a house in Weymouth for the season?" went on the irrepressible young woman. "It's so gay when the Royal Family are in residence, but as dull as anything could be during the winter months! And my husband will never go to London — so tiresome of him, don't you agree? But just now it's all delightful, what with visitors galore and the military — though to be sure one is frightened to death by all this talk of an invasion!" She paused for breath, then gave Emma a dazzling smile. "If you're to come here often, ma'am, I may as well make myself known to you, for I haunt the place, don't I Berenice?"

Berenice was heard to murmur that Madam was indeed a most valued client.

"Well, one must fill the time somehow — there's so much of it, don't you agree, ma'am? But pray allow me to introduce myself — my name's Kitty Melbury. My husband's Ralph Melbury of Mayne House, which is between Poyntz Ferrers and Bincombe — but I dare say it won't mean anything to you, as you're a stranger to these parts."

"On the contrary," replied Emma with a smile, "I do at least have some small acquaintance with Poyntz Ferrers, for my husband and I are staying at Poyntz Manor for a few months. I am Emma Wynford. How d'you do?"

"Poyntz Manor! How delightful! When I heard that it was to be let again, I feared that it would be taken by yet another elderly couple here for health reasons, like the last tenants. Well, it's capital to find that you're of an age with myself, Mrs. Wynford — do, pray, let us be friends."

She put out her hand with an impulsive gesture and Emma took it, reminded for a moment of Antonia's easy, friendly approach.

"May we call on you soon?" continued Kitty Melbury. "My husband is never backward in such matters — he likes to make the acquaintance of new arrivals. Not that we have many in our immediate neighbourhood, sad to say! But our house is always full of company, thank goodness, for I don't like to be too much alone, do you? Now, do say that we may wait on you at Poyntz Manor soon!"

Emma replied that she and Mr. Wynford would be very happy to see their neighbours, hoping fervently that this was true. Would Rupert Wynford find this acquaintance desirable? But then he must realise that it was the custom in country districts to visit newcomers; besides, he had spoken only yesterday of his intention to mix freely in local society.

Mrs. Melbury took her leave with further expressions of friendship and Emma was soon able to re-join Wynford in the showroom. They were on the point of leaving when the door of the shop opened to admit a man who certainly did not look like a customer. He was dressed in the serviceable suit of brown fustian much worn by the ordinary citizens, and even this homely attire looked dusty and travel-stained. He began to say something, but Madame Tiffany cut him short, her black eyes snapping with anger.

"You'll find a tradesman's entrance at the rear of the shop — round the corner and down the alley a few yards."

Considerably abashed, he knuckled his forehead and withdrew.

"A female I wouldn't care to cross," commented Wynford, as they returned to the waiting carriage. "He'd come some way by the look of him, poor devil, wouldn't you say?"

Emma agreed absentmindedly, then went on to tell him of her meeting with Kitty Melbury.

"Ralph Melbury?" he said. "Yes, I know of him — local squire, very hospitable, by all accounts, knows everybody in the district. This is his second marriage, to a lady from Bath about thirty years younger than himself. Pretty, silly, hen-witted creature, so I hear. But by all means cultivate her acquaintance, if you wish, as long as you're discreet. It will be good for you to have some female companionship, besides helping to bring us more speedily into local society. I've one or two casual acquaintances in Weymouth, but it won't do to rely entirely on them."

She wondered a little at his knowledge of the Melburys, in spite of never having met them, but did not risk a question for fear of a snub. Most likely this, too, was information which he had no intention of disclosing to her.

NINE

They spent the rest of the morning walking on the Esplanade among all the people of fashion. The sun was warm, but not too hot, tempered by a soft breeze from the sea. Out in the bay several frigates could be seen, a reminder of the ever-present threat of invasion from the French. But Emma was not in the mood for such gloomy thoughts; even the doubts and fears of the previous night had been swept away. She strolled along the handsome semi-circular walk on Wynford's arm, enjoying the sunshine and the fresh tang of the sea, looking about her with a lively interest, and from time to time smiling up into his face at some amusing remark he made. He could certainly be an interesting and charming companion when he chose. He pointed out Gloucester Lodge, where the Royal Family would be staying when they arrived in Weymouth, and the Assembly rooms at the Royal Hotel.

"That reminds me," he said, in a confidential tone, "one of the things I ought to know about you, but don't, is if you're fond of dancing? There are frequent balls at the Rooms here, and we must attend some of them."

Emma looked dubious. "It's some time since I attended a ball, but I don't think I've quite forgotten the dance steps. I trust I'll be able to do you credit."

"Never fear," he answered, smiling down at her. "It's like swimming — once mastered, one never loses the knack, so they say."

"I don't know about that, as I can't swim."

"Another fact for my notebook — but I should have guessed that you might not. How many females do, I wonder? Still, you may have the opportunity to learn here, if you wish. The Royal Family take a dip most mornings when they're in residence here — at the ungodly hour of six."

"Six o'clock!" gasped Emma. "How monstrous!"

He laughed. "Why, so I think. But, all the same, we must make the effort to come down here some morning so that you may enjoy the spectacle of so many fashionable people astir at an hour when they would normally be in their beds, sound asleep."

"I suppose there's no saying what people will do when Royalty leads the way."

"No, indeed." He broke off to give her arm a warning squeeze, saying, "Here come some acquaintances of mine — needless to say, they are not in our secret, so be on your guard."

She looked up with a slight quickening of her pulse. There had been several military and Volunteer uniforms among the crowd which had been passing around them; but now she noticed three officers in particular who were approaching in company with two ladies.

"Hah, Wynford!" The speaker was a blond, thick-set man in his early thirties, wearing the insignia of a captain. "Taking the air, what? When did you return to Weymouth, my dear fellow? Saw you here a few months back with that dashed pretty sister of yours, then you vanished again! Regular Jack in the box, that's what!"

Wynford made some suitable reply, and introductions followed. Captain Gill's wife was a rather plain, staid looking young woman who had very little to say for herself. The other two officers were Lieutenants, younger than the Captain. One of them, Lieutenant Tilley, had the attractive, devil-may-care look which Emma had often seen in some of the young officers whom her father had brought home occasionally in the old days. The other was introduced as Lieutenant Lester; his wife was a dainty little woman with soft auburn hair. Unlike Mrs. Gill, she scarcely ever stopped talking, and seemed to be laughing a good deal with Lieutenant Tilley at very little, while her husband looked somewhat moodily on; or so Emma thought. But then, the Lieutenant was obviously the kind of young man who would be very attractive to women, and most likely he knew it.

The newcomers joined Emma and Wynford in strolling about the Esplanade. The party tended after a while to separate into sexes, and Emma found herself carrying on an animated conversation with Mrs. Lester to which Mrs. Gill would occasionally contribute a reluctant remark.

"So you've only just arrived, Mrs. Wynford," said Mrs. Lester, after the usual comments on the weather and the pleasantness of Weymouth at this season had been made. "Do you find your house agreeable?"

"Oh, yes," replied Emma. "I'm so glad that no one has thought to modernise it, for Tudor panelling is very much to my taste."

"Oh, well, if you like that kind of thing, but for myself I prefer the classical style — so much lighter and more cheerful. Don't you agree, Mrs. Gill?"

Mrs. Gill looked as though she would much rather not have been applied to but gave it as her opinion that there was something to be said for both.

"Well, we have a lodging in the town," went on Mrs. Lester, without listening properly to her companion. "And it's the dreariest hole imaginable! But, of course, it isn't in one of the fashionable streets. We're such birds of passage, we military men's wives — never in any place for long enough to make a settled home. I suppose you have a house in London, Mrs. Wynford?"

"Yes," replied Emma, thinking quickly of a way to turn the subject, as she did not relish being questioned too closely on this one. "But we're fixed here for some months, so I'm glad I like Poyntz Manor so much. By the way, do either of you ladies know a Mrs. Melbury, of Mayne House? I encountered her at a gown shop this morning, and she promised to call on us."

Mrs. Lester laughed. "Oh, yes, Kitty Melbury! Indeed, she invites half the neighbourhood to her house, so you couldn't find a more useful person for introducing you to local society. She's a lively girl enough, but her husband's a dull stick, to my way of thinking, and I don't believe theirs is a happy marriage."

Emma had no relish for gossip, so she failed to follow up this remark; but Mrs. Lester needed no encouragement to continue.

"She never *says* anything, of course, though she and I are by way of being friends since my husband's been quartered here; but one can soon read between the lines, don't you think? She goes away a good deal and he never goes with her; and for all that they are constantly entertaining company at Mayne House, they don't seem to have any close friends. He treats her rather as though she were a backward child, but then he's at least thirty years her senior."

"Have they no children?" asked Emma.

"Oh, no; but then they have only been two years married, so there's plenty of time for that. We have no family, either. Have you, Mrs. Wynford?" Emma shook her head. "Oh, dear, perhaps I ought not to have asked," continued Mrs. Lester, with a sudden pretence of contrition. "I did hear from Captain Gill that Mr. Wynford had brought you to Weymouth for your health, and, naturally, I wondered —" She broke off and looked at Emma, who felt a faint blush starting, much to her annoyance.

"There, I shouldn't have spoken!" exclaimed Mrs. Lester, in a gloating tone. "When you know me better, you may perhaps confide in me."

Emma thought this unlikely, even if the circumstances had been more normal. Mrs. Gill looked uncomfortable, and put in one of her remarks, thus succeeding in changing the subject. Not long afterwards, the party broke up to go their separate ways; but not before Captain Gill had engaged them all to dine at his house that evening.

"Well, what did you think of the ladies?" asked Wynford, as they were driving home together.

"They're in great contrast to each other," she said, with a laugh. "One talks all the time and the other never utters a syllable if she can help it. Not but what," she added fairly, "she did come to my rescue on one occasion, when Mrs. Lester was prying a trifle too much."

"Oh?" His tone was sharp.

She recounted the episode, and he nodded, relieved. "Yes, well, it's easy to see what she was driving at, but nothing that need alarm us, thank God. She has the reputation of being a rattle, but I don't think there's any real harm in her. At least — " He paused, frowning.

She waited a moment to see if he wished to add anything; then said, "There's always a certain amount of harm in gossip, don't you think? She was trying to tell me that my new acquaintance, Mrs. Melbury, wasn't happy in her marriage. I shouldn't relish anyone speaking so of my affairs to a total stranger!"

"Ah, well, your kind of marriage is the best of all," he said, with a cynical twist of his lips. "A purely financial arrangement that can be concluded at any time. But pray tell me exactly what she said about the Melburys."

Emma felt surprised at his interest in what had probably been only feline gossip, but she dutifully repeated Mrs. Lester's remarks.

"Judging by what you saw of Mrs. Melbury yourself, do you think there's anything in it?" he asked.

She stared. "How do you expect me to answer that, Mr. Wynford? We only spoke together for ten minutes at the most. But I did gain the impression that she finds her life trivial and boring. She spoke of too much time on her hands and that she was always in and out of the gown shop. But you won't wish to concern yourself with such matters," she added, quickly, fearing a snub.

"On the contrary, my dear. One of the ways in which you can particularly serve me is to bring me all the tattle you may hear in your dealings with the females hereabouts."

"As you wish," she said, scornfully, "but pray don't blame me if you find it tedious. Must I then repeat every conversation with another female? Some of them may be so trivial I shall scarcely recollect them afterwards!"

"Ah, your professional training will stand you in good stead there. But what I want to know is anything that touches on the way of life of our neighbours, on their relationships with each other. You may safely leave me to sort the grain from the chaff."

"So I'm to act the spy, now!"

"A dual role," he agreed, gravely, then burst out laughing at her disgusted expression. "What a little Miss Prunes and Prisms you are at times, Emma, to be sure! Or is that another of your acts, I wonder?"

Fortunately, he seemed to credit her with acting when she was only being natural; she was too relieved at this to take offence at the rest of his speech. But the doubts that had receded earlier in the evening now began to creep back again. Surely there could never be any justification for an honest man to behave in this way?

The evening at Captain Gill's proved less of a strain for her than she had feared. Already she was beginning to adjust to her changed circumstances and to take her place once more as an equal in genteel society. The Captain's wife was a good hostess, although she was no more talkative in her own home than she had been on the Esplanade. Perhaps her husband talked enough for both of them, thought Emma. As for Mrs. Lester, she was even more voluble than before, laughing a good deal and rolling her provocative green eyes at each of the gentlemen in turn. Emma began positively to dislike the woman; there was always a touch of malice in everything she said.

Towards the end of the evening, Emma chanced to be sitting beside Lieutenant Tilley, and they began to chat to each other.

He was a good-looking young man, tall and slim, with brown hair brushed into a fashionable Brutus style, a determined chin, and blue eyes which frequently held a twinkle. He told her that at present he was in command of a signal station at White Nothe, a few miles east of Osmington Mills.

"That sounds very important," said Emma. "Though I must confess that I'm not perfectly sure what a signal station is."

"My dear ma'am!" He flung up his hands in horror, thereby attracting the notice of Rupert Wynford, who was at that moment talking to the other two men and Mrs. Lester in a group a little way apart. "One of our most essential coastal defences, and you don't even know what it is! And I understand from Captain Gill that your husband was once an Army man, which makes it worse!"

She laughed at his mock indignation, wondering for a moment how true it really was that Rupert Wynford had been in the Army and had sold out. It was certainly part of the biography which he had prepared for her to learn; and it could be the truth, since he had already been acquainted with Captain Gill, though not, she thought, very well.

"I quite see I am sunk beyond reproach by my admission, but I am very willing to learn."

"Oh, not quite beyond reproach," he replied, giving her a calculated look of admiration from his expressive blue eyes. "I can't find it in my heart to be too severe upon you, ma'am, when you look at me in that disarming way."

She smiled tolerantly, dismissing his nonsense. A sparkle came into his eyes as though he had accepted a challenge.

"Well, I will enlighten you — that is, if you really want to know, but it's tedious stuff with which to entertain a pretty young woman."

Emma laughed lightly. "I am always made suspicious by flattery, let me warn you, sir! But I would like to know, all the same."

"Ah, but it wasn't flattery," he countered, quickly. "But I see your husband has his eye on us, and no doubt will presently call me out, if I'm not more careful. I will talk to you very seriously, now, I promise. There are a number of signal stations at various points along the coast for the purpose of passing messages in the event of a visit from our friends across the Channel."

Emma wrinkled her brow. "Passing messages — but how, exactly?"

"By means of signals in a code which represents numbers, and also certain words and phrases. There are sixty-three possible combinations, shown by white dots on shutters painted black. A framework is set up on the roof of the signal station, and the various shutters are cranked up to this from the room beneath."

"How ingenious! But surely the signals can't be seen from any great distance?"

"The range of vision's about twelve miles on a clear day — that's with a telescope, of course. There's always a man on duty with a telescope at every station."

"It must be very tedious work," said Emma.

He shrugged. "The men take it in turns. But yes, it is tedious — and remote, stuck up there on a hill top, away from all the rest of the world." He gave her a provocative glance. "I much prefer my present situation, assure you."

"One can see that quite well, Tilley."

Emma started a little on hearing Wynford's voice close beside her. Looking up, she saw that he was standing behind them, leaning slightly over the back of the sofa she and Lieutenant Tilley were sharing.

"And who shall blame you," he went on, with an indulgent smile. "Certainly not myself. But come, Emma, my love, it's time we started back. If we are to put the roses into those cheeks again —" here he leaned over and gently pinched Emma's cheek in a proprietorial way that made her seethe inwardly — "we must not have too many late nights."

Lieutenant Tilley stood up, making a little bow in Emma's direction. "You know best, of course, Wynford; but you must allow me to say that Mrs. Wynford looks in the bloom of health."

Wynford's glance moved from Emma's hair, glinting gold in the candlelight, to the curve of her lips, there he allowed it to rest.

"Ah, yes, my dear chap," he murmured. "But then, you do not know her as well as I do."

She contained herself until they were seated in the carriage on their way back to Poyntz Ferrers, and then her indignation broke loose.

"I must say I do not think it at all necessary for you to be so — so odiously possessive, sir!"

"What is a husband supposed to do when he sees his wife flirting with another man?" he asked, reasonably.

Emma's face reddened. "I was not flirting! I was merely making myself agreeable!"

"More agreeable than you choose to make yourself to me," he replied, in a tone she could not quite fathom.

"Yes, well — ours is a business relationship, as you have reminded me many times. I can never behave naturally with you, for we must always be acting a part. But as long as I don't betray our secret, I may surely be more or less natural with others?"

"If you consider it natural behaviour for a woman who has been less than two years married, to encourage another man to flirt with her."

"Once again, I tell you I did *not* encourage him! It was all his nonsense, anyway — I am quite accustomed to young officers of his stamp. I used to meet with them frequently at one time."

"When they came backstage, I presume?" asked Wynford, with an edge to his tone.

She was about to deny this hotly, but checked herself suddenly, remembering. He noticed her hesitation, and a frown wrinkled his brows.

"Let me understand you," said Emma, in a calmer tone. "Are you complaining that I played my part badly?"

He said nothing for a moment, still frowning. "Oh, for God's sake!" he exclaimed impatiently, at last. "No — not exactly that. But if I'm to play mine successfully, I must show some signs of jealousy when a young coxcomb makes up to you. So if you dislike my attentions, you know what to do in order to avoid them for the future. And now let's forget the whole stupid business."

"Willingly," said Emma, with dignity.

TEN

There was no sign of Rupert Wynford on the following morning, so after a solitary breakfast Emma went outside to explore the grounds. There was a small rose garden close to the house, with a lily pond where a fountain played. She sat beside the pond on a shady bench for some time, yielding to the simple pleasure of watching running water in the sunlight.

At length she roused herself to complete her tour. Apart from a thriving kitchen garden where an elderly man and a boy were working, the rest was given over to lawns, trees and a modest orchard of apples and pears.

She thought that by now Wynford might be looking for her, so returned to the house, only to be informed by the housekeeper that he had ridden out at a very early hour and had not yet returned.

"I dare say he wouldn't care to disturb you, ma'am, to tell you of it," Mrs. Hinton suggested.

Emma nodded. "Most likely. Well, I think I shall take a short stroll around the village, so perhaps you'll be good enough to mention that I'll be back soon, should he return before I do."

Mrs. Hinton agreed to this; and Emma, stopping only to fetch her parasol, walked down the drive and into a lane.

She stood in the shade of the willows beside the village pond, looking about her. The small stone footbridge invited her to cross it, yet it led only to the cottages which could just as easily be reached by a turning off the lane at the other end of the pond. She gave in to the whim, strolling past cottage doors set open to the sun and catching glimpses of neat parlours within. She re-joined the lane to walk a little farther and discover a mill. She stood for a moment, idly watching the wheel turning and the rush of waters. A sense of peace pervaded her. This was a quiet, well ordered village, nestling securely in the shelter of its encircling green hills; what right had Rupert Wynford to disturb its peace with his sinister fantasies?

She sighed and started back towards the Manor. As she came to the turning by the pond, a slender figure in a green walking dress was approaching from that direction.

"Oh, Mrs. Wynford!" It was Kitty Melbury, stretching out an impetuous hand in welcome. "How truly delightful to meet you — are you walking alone?"

Emma took the hand, smiling. "Why, yes. My husband chanced to be from home this morning, so I came out to get a closer look at the village. It's charming, is it not?"

"Well, I suppose so," replied Kitty Melbury doubtfully. "To be sure, it's picturesque enough, but it's so very *quiet*, don't you know? Nothing ever happens here — not like Weymouth, though that's dull enough in the winter months. If it were not for entertaining a good deal, and going away frequently on visits, I declare I should be moped to death! But as you're here for only a few months, you'll probably like it well enough, I dare say. Anyway, I mustn't disenchant you."

"Are you walking for pleasure?" asked Emma, thinking it better to pass over these remarks. "Or are you bound on a particular errand?"

"Oh, no, nothing in particular, only that I grew tired of my own company. I had hoped to persuade my husband to call on you this morning, but he had to go out on some business matters."

"And mine is not at home at present," said Emma, "so if you care to accompany me back to the house, we can entertain each other for a while."

Kitty readily agreed, and soon the two were sitting together in the small morning room where Emma had breakfasted. They had not been there for more than ten minutes when Wynford came into the room. He was dressed for riding; his boots showed traces of dust from the roads, and a dishevelled lock of hair fell over his forehead. He smoothed it back hastily on seeing a stranger there with Emma.

"I beg your pardon, my dear — I didn't know you had company," he apologised.

"May I present my husband to you?" Emma said to Kitty. "This lady is Mrs. Melbury from Mayne House, Mr. Wynford. You may recall my mentioning that I had met her at Madame Tiffany's."

The two acknowledged the introduction, taking stock of each other.

"Beg you'll excuse my dirt, ma'am," said Wynford, smoothly. "I had not thought of finding company, or I'd have stopped to clean up a trifle. If you'll forgive me, I'll re-join you in a few minutes."

He bowed himself out. Kitty stared after him thoughtfully.

"Have you been married long, Mrs. Wynford? Oh, forgive me, perhaps I shouldn't ask!"

"Why should you not?" replied Emma, calmly. "Yes, we've been married for close on two years."

Kitty sighed. "And I for several months more. Is it not melancholy to reflect that we are quite old married women?"

"As to that," replied Emma, laughing, "I wouldn't consider myself qualified for such a title on the strength of two years' marriage."

"No, but it's easy to see that you and Mr. Wynford are happy together," remarked Kitty, wistfully.

"How can you say so, after seeing us in company for only a moment?"

"Something — I don't know exactly — something in the way he looked at you —"

Emma laughed again to hide her embarrassment, and quickly turned the conversation into less personal channels. But the comment nagged at her on the second level of her thoughts. Could it be that her employer was feeling a more personal interest in her? She reminded herself sharply that, if so, she had better discourage it. To him she was an actress, a woman outside his own sphere, and any proposals he might make her would certainly not be of marriage.

He re-joined them presently and sat listening to Kitty Melbury's chatter with every appearance of enjoyment. When she said she thought she ought to go, he offered at once to escort her home in the carriage and refused to listen to her polite protestations.

"You are too good, Mr. Wynford. And if you do come, I hope you will stay for a few minutes to make my husband's acquaintance. He will most likely have finished his tiresome business by now and would be delighted to see you both."

To reach Mayne House, they took the turning by the pond, which came out into a road winding steeply uphill towards Bincombe. The distance, as Mrs. Melbury had told Emma, was only about half a mile, so they were soon turning into the gates and drawing up before a house in the prevailing Dorset stone.

Pressed by Kitty Melbury, they were shown into a parlour on the ground floor, where their hostess left them to go in search of her husband.

"How did you happen to be together?" asked Wynford, in a low tone. "Did she call on you?"

Emma just had time to explain that they had met in the village when Kitty Melbury returned with her husband.

Ralph Melbury was a distinguished looking man in his early fifties; judging from his upright carriage and shrewd eye, he would be something of a sportsman, Wynford thought. He greeted his visitors affably, rang for refreshment, and was soon deep in conversation with Wynford on sporting topics and horseflesh.

After sitting together for half an hour, Wynford looked at his watch and said they must be going.

"We shall hope to see you again soon," said Ralph Melbury, cordially. "Some of our neighbours are to dine here on Friday — I wonder, now, would you and Mrs. Wynford care to join us? No doubt you will wish to become acquainted with the local gentry, even if you are not to stay among us for long."

"Oh, yes, pray do come!" Kitty turned a face alight with enthusiasm towards Emma. "You need not fear it will be too large a party for you to get to know everybody, and they are all very friendly. There are the Warhams from Osmington — she's a middle-aged lady with a grown-up family, and so kind! Then there are the Rivers from Preston — he's a Captain in the Volunteers and they have four young children. Such darlings! And the Shirleys are coming from Bincombe — I always enjoy Mrs. Shirley's company, she is such fun! And, of course," her voice dropped away a little, "the Reverend George Bredy and his wife from Littlemore."

Emma looked towards Wynford for guidance, a fact which Ralph Melbury noted with a slightly ironical smile.

"Delighted, I'm sure," Rupert Wynford bowed. "Very good of you to invite us."

"Not at all — a pleasure. Will half after six suit you?"

This was agreed and the visitors took their departure.

"Entirely satisfactory," remarked Wynford, as they settled themselves in the carriage. "It was perhaps scarce worth ordering out the carriage for such a paltry journey, but one can't make an omelette without breaking eggs, I believe."

Emma stared at him. "Do you mean to say that you offered Mrs. Melbury a lift home in order to gain admittance to their house?"

"Indeed I do. Oh, she would have asked us there at some time, I know, but this did hasten the process," he replied carelessly.

"Upon my word, it's difficult to know what you would be at!" exclaimed Emma, in disgust. "Everything is calculated with you — nothing is spontaneous!"

He raised his eyebrows in mild surprise. "But of course. You are well aware that I am here for a definite purpose and not merely for idle pleasure."

"I wish I knew what that purpose was. I don't mind admitting that at times I am made very uneasy by all this mystery." A note of pleading crept into her voice. "Can you not enlighten me — please?"

He shook his head decidedly. "No — perhaps later, but certainly not at present. You do your part, and I will take care of mine. No more on that subject now —" as she looked about to argue — "or you will put me out of temper. A wise wife is careful never to do that to her spouse. These people whom we shall be meeting there the day after tomorrow —" he went on, changing the subject abruptly. "The Melbury female told you something about them, but perhaps I should fill in the gaps in your knowledge, so that you'll know what to expect, and where to be most on your guard. Lady Warham is a motherly kind of woman, and as such may represent more of a hazard to you than the others, for you may feel an urge to confide in her at some time. I need scarcely say that you must suppress it. Mrs. Rivers will bore you with endless stories of her children. Mrs. Bredy, the clergyman's wife, will most likely ignore you; she's a social snob of the worst type, besides being a vain, extravagant female who spends far more than her husband's stipend can possibly provide. One wonders just where she gets the rest, for she has no private source of income as far as is known. Mrs. Shirley is innocuous enough — lively and sociable, always well dressed, another good customer of Madame Tiffany."

"But if you've never met these people before," said Emma, amazed, "how on earth can you know so much about them?"

"I have my methods. But I must mention, my dear Emma, that you are allowing yourself to fall into a deplorable wifely habit of asking too many questions. Pray curb it, I beg. I don't find it at all endearing."

ELEVEN

Emma was due to visit Madame Tiffany's for a fitting on the following afternoon, and somewhat to her surprise Wynford offered to accompany her.

"I quite thought you would have been put off by your previous visit," she remarked, with a laugh. "I fear it was prodigiously expensive!"

He shrugged. "As wives go, your demands are quite moderate. But I don't propose to come into the shop with you on this occasion, as I've a commission of my own to execute. If you will fix a time when you'll be ready, I'll be waiting to escort you home."

He conducted her to Madame Tiffany's and dismissed the coachman until the appointed time of return, then sauntered into the next street to find the alley which gave access to the rear of the shops. Having located this, he gave a sharp look along it to make sure that no one was about at the moment.

His luck was in; he turned along the alley, pausing outside the door which he had calculated would give access to Madame Tiffany's premises. His scrutiny proved disappointing. The windows at the rear were naturally much smaller than those at the front of the shop, and were so closely curtained that it was impossible to catch even the faintest glimpse of the interior. The door was firmly shut.

He reminded himself that an unseen watcher behind those discreet curtains would have the advantage of him, so he did not linger there, but walked on at a leisurely pace.

He had almost reached the other end of the alley, which was short, when his sharp ears caught the sound of a bolt being drawn back from a door somewhere behind him. Quickly concealing himself as best he could behind a pile of rubbish outside one of the doors he was passing, he peered back in the direction he had come.

He was in time to see a man emerge from Madame Tiffany's door, walk the short distance to the opposite end of the alley and turn into the street beyond.

Wynford started in pursuit, treading catlike over the uneven cobbles and keeping an eye open for anyone who might be watching him from a window. He appeared to be unobserved, however, as far as he could tell; reaching the end of the alley, he scanned the street in the direction his quarry had taken. There were few people about at the time, and Wynford soon sighted the man he wanted, making his way down the street in the direction of the harbour.

He followed at a discreet distance. The man reached the harbour and turned into a tavern on the quay called The Ship.

Wynford hesitated a moment before following. So far, he had seen his quarry only from the rear, but he was anxious to get a look at the man's face. On the other hand, he had no wish to draw attention to himself from that quarter. A quick glance inside showed that the place was crowded, however, so he edged his way inside.

It took a few minutes to locate his man; but at last Wynford saw him leaning against the counter, on which he had just flung down the price of a tankard of ale. A little careful manoeuvring gave a quick glimpse of the other's face without being exposed to view himself.

It was enough to confirm his suspicions. This was the same man who had angered Madame Tiffany the other day by bursting into her showroom instead of using the tradesman's entrance. It seemed he had not learnt better, a fact which Wynford found interesting.

Wynford elbowed his way out of the crowded tap-room and walked along the quay to a capstan at a short distance from The Ship. Perching himself on this, legs outstretched in the indolent attitude of one who has time to kill, he stared idly at the boats bobbing about in the harbour.

Out of the corner of his eye, he saw the man emerge presently from The Ship and begin to stroll along the quay. His eyes, too, were fixed upon the boats, but with rather more purpose than Wynford was showing. A short distance beyond the capstan, he suddenly gave a signal to one of the rowing boats. The oarsman responded and began to bring his boat in to a flight of steps farther along the quay. Having reached these, Wynford's quarry descended and climbed into the boat, which pulled out again into the harbour and was soon lost to view.

Rupert Wynford consulted his watch. There was nothing more to be done at present, but as he had been warned, Madame Tiffany's shop would repay surveillance. That must be seen to without undue delay. In the meantime, he had one more task to perform before meeting Emma.

He turned back into the town with a quickened step and entered a fashionable jeweller's shop. Emerging some time later, he hastened to his rendezvous to arrive just as Emma was leaving Madame Tiffany's premises. At the same moment, the coach turned into the street.

"Well, was it all satisfactory?" he asked, once they were seated.

"Oh, yes, thank you, all went splendidly! And I am to have three of the gowns delivered this evening, in time for me to wear one of them at the Melburys' tomorrow, and a riding dress, besides. The proprietress said that she will deliver the complete order by the end of the week, which is prodigiously quick, do you not think? She must have a veritable army of seamstresses to work for her, or she couldn't possibly do it."

"Is it too much to hope that one of the three may be that shimmering blue creation which she showed us the other day?"

"You mean the blue silk under gauze?" She looked at him curiously. "Yes, as it happens, it is. Why do you ask, sir?"

"Come, come, Emma, how many times must I remind you not to address me in that way? 'Mr. Wynford' if you must — 'my dear' or 'my love' occasionally for the benefit of others — but never that formal 'sir'! It won't do at all."

"I'm sorry. But why," she persisted, "did you want to know if I would have the blue gown?"

"Because it became you so well," he replied, smiling down at her. "And also I was fascinated by the way in which it changed the colour of your eyes from grey to blue."

She felt a blush rising, and turned away hastily, making some remark about the view from the carriage window.

Later that evening, when the gowns arrived from the shop, Emma held the blue one up against her before the long mirror.

Yes, undoubtedly, it did change the colour of her eyes. She had known once that certain colours did have this effect, but the knowledge had been forgotten in the past years of austere, governessy dressing.

Matilda exclaimed in rapture. "Oh, ma'am, what a lovely gown and how well you'll look in it, for sure! Will you try them on, ma'am, before you dress for dinner?"

Emma agreed that it would be as well, in case there should be any alteration needed; so the abigail helped her out of the walking dress she was wearing and slipped on the new blue one. It was cut in the prevailing classical style, low-necked, high waisted, with tiny puff sleeves and a loosely flowing skirt. Emma gazed at herself in the mirror, Narcissus-like, and could scarcely believe that this was the staid governess who had walked desolately into the Crown only a few weeks since.

But then she was not that same person, she reflected. People change with changing circumstances, and she knew she could never again return to what she once had been. She smoothed the gown with her fingers while Matilda twittered admiringly in the background, and her thoughts turned to what Rupert Wynford had said. Strange that he should have noticed so much about her, since he never deviated from their business-like relationship unless they were in company. She felt herself blushing again, and reminded herself sharply that he was, after all, a man of keen observation.

She was immersed in these thoughts when a gentle tap sounded on the communicating door. She started as if it had been a thunderous knock and spun round to face that way.

"May I come in?"

It was Wynford's voice. For a moment she hesitated, then realised that she could not refuse with Matilda there to wonder at it. Besides, the maid's presence would relieve the situation of any embarrassment. All the same, her throat was dry as she assented.

He came into the room at once, closing the door quietly behind him, then stood for a moment looking at her without speaking.

Matilda bobbed a curtsey and started to withdraw.

"Oh, no!" cried Emma, on a note of desperation, making a gesture towards the abigail. "Pray, don't go, Matilda — I — we — I shall need you to help me on with the other gowns!"

Wynford smiled cajolingly. "A moment only, my love. I have brought you something."

He nodded to Matilda in dismissal, and she left them alone. Emma's eyes turned on the closing door with an expression almost of panic.

"Something for me?" she repeated, breathlessly.

He nodded, and she noticed now that he kept his left hand hidden behind his back. "A surprise," he said, still smiling. "Turn around, Emma, to face the mirror, and close your eyes. Tightly, mind."

She obeyed, hardly knowing what she was doing in her present confusion. She felt his fingers lightly touch her neck as he placed something about it. After a moment, he said, "Now look."

She opened her eyes and saw that she was wearing a delicately worked pendant necklace of sapphires and diamonds set in gold. Wynford stooped to lay a pair of matching earrings on her dressing table.

"These you must put on for yourself," he said. "The task is beyond my skill. Turn around, Emma, and let me see you."

She obeyed, putting an unsteady hand up to the necklace. "But — but I can't possibly take this jewellery," she stammered. "I — truly I cannot!"

"Why not? Don't you like them? Of course, I should have consulted your taste first, but I wanted it to be a surprise." He sounded disappointed. "We can change them, however, for something else, in the morning, if you wish."

"But I don't wish!" Her senses were returning now, and with them her usual fluency of speech. "When I say I can't accept them, you know well what I mean. They are far too expensive!"

He appeared to consider this. "Oh, I don't know about that. Anything cheaper would be shabby, don't you agree? Confound it, a man must give his wife creditable jewellery, or else be known for a skinflint."

She made no answer, but in spite of herself had a struggle not to smile.

"Well, I must say," he continued, in a gentle, martyr-like tone, "I had looked for some show of pleasure. Perhaps even a little — a very little, mark you — gratitude. But possibly I expected too much."

She caught the twinkle in his eye.

"I — oh!" she exclaimed, in exasperation. "You twist everything so that I appear in the wrong!"

"Do I? Well I realise that I am a reprehensible creature," he admitted, laughing. He sobered quickly, gazing at her with a warmth of expression that quickened Emma's pulses. "You are very lovely, Emma," he said, in an altered tone. "Do you realise that?"

His hands came out to rest gently on her shoulders. For a moment she stood quite still. He made as if to draw her closer, but with a sudden movement she jerked herself free. Countless emotions were warring within her at that moment; but the one she allowed mastery was anger.

"So this is the way you keep your word not to exploit the situation," she said icily. "You have spoken all along as though you considered me no better than I ought to be, and I suppose you thought these trinkets were my price. Well, now you know you are mistaken — here, take them, for I shall never wear them!"

She unfastened the necklace, and, seizing the earrings, thrust the jewels back at him.

He ignored her outstretched hands. His face hardened.

"You're mistaken, ma'am — you *will* wear them," he said in a tone of command.

"Never!" Her chin went up in defiance and her cheeks were flushed.

"You will do as I say, because that is part of our contract." His tone now was as cold as hers. "You are acting the role of my wife, and as such must appear before the world in suitable style. If you choose to think of these trinkets as mere stage properties, like the clothes you are wearing, that is your affair. I purchased them for a very different reason — but not the one you so readily impute to me. But since that gift was unacceptable to you, possibly this will find more favour, since you yourself asked for it. Here it is. I need scarcely say that you must use it with discretion, so that the servants don't notice."

He pulled something from his pocket and tossed it contemptuously on the dressing table, where it landed with a metallic ring. Then he strode from the bedchamber into his own, slamming the door.

Emma stood for a moment looking after him, then sank on to the stool before the dressing table, letting the jewels drop from her hands. She took up the object he had flung down.

It was a key.

TWELVE

The Melburys provided their guests with an excellent dinner; and, judging by the length of time the gentlemen spent afterwards sitting over the wine, that was equally satisfactory. Emma, meanwhile, was improving her acquaintance with the ladies of the party in the drawing room.

"So you have not been too well lately, Mrs. Wynford," Lady Warham said to her, in a kindly tone. "I trust you will soon find the change of air beneficial. Do you mean to try sea-bathing? The Royal Family go in almost every day when they are in Weymouth, and it is said that the Princesses find it of great benefit."

"Doctor West recommended it for my Charles last summer," put in Mrs. Rivers, a dark-haired woman in her late thirties, with a permanently worried expression. "Charles is more delicate than the others, I fear, though, to be sure, Mary and Little Arabella aren't very strong. But one expects a boy to be more robust than girls, and Bertram — my eldest, you know, Mrs. Wynford — is really quite sturdy. I felt some anxiety about his chest when he was younger, but he really does seem much stronger these days, thank Heavens."

"You worry too much my dear," put in Lady Warham gently. "Children do have these little ups and downs, but they usually grow out of them."

"For my part," said Mrs. Shirley, with a laugh, "I think they are better for a little healthy neglect."

"Ah, but yours are boys, Charlotte," said Mrs. Rivers, "and they never gave you the least anxiety, did they, when they were little? Although you must often worry now that they're away at school, wondering if they get enough to eat, or if the discipline is too harsh."

"Not a bit of it!" replied Charlotte Shirley, cheerfully. "If their father managed to survive Winchester, I imagine so will they."

Mrs. Shirley was about the same age as Mrs. Rivers, but the two women were very different in both looks and temperament. Charlotte Shirley was a blonde, with a good figure, attractive features and a gay, easy manner which soon put her on good terms with strangers; tense and anxious, Jane Rivers seemed unable to forget her own problems for long enough to take an interest in those of anyone else. Nevertheless, Emma wondered if Mrs. Shirley was really interested in anyone other than herself.

"Well, I may perhaps go into the sea," she answered Lady Warham. "But I am very much better now, I thank you."

"They do look so *frightful*, don't they?" put in Mrs. Bredy, who had been flicking over the pages of a fashion magazine, disdaining to join in such a boring conversation.

"Who? The females in the Lady's Magazine?" asked Kitty Melbury, puzzled.

"No, not that, though there are one or two rather odd fashions," drawled Mrs. Bredy, patting a stray curl into place. "I shall certainly not have them copied. No, I meant the bathers — that odious garment, so like a shroud, which one must wear — and then one's hair, you know! There can be no doing anything with it afterwards — so shaming!"

"Mine always goes up into tight curls, just like a baby's!" laughed Kitty.

"Well, if you will favour that Titus cut," retorted Mrs. Bredy, "I don't at all care for the style myself, though I admit —" grudgingly — "that it suits you well enough."

"I think it looks charming on dear Kitty," said Lady Warham, with a look of reproach at the elegant Mrs. Bredy.

Emma agreed with this, and Kitty, in her usual volatile way launched into a long account of the various styles in which she had dressed her hair over the past few years. Emma only just succeeded in stifling a yawn and wished the gentlemen would join them. At least it would give the conversation a new turn.

She had seen very little of Rupert Wynford since the incident yesterday in her bedchamber. He had spent the evening away from home after an almost silent meal together; and he had been out of the house for most of today. She reflected that they would need to appear amicable together this evening, whatever their individual feelings might be. It would not do for the neighbours to suspect that the Wynfords had quarrelled.

He came into the room with the others almost as the wish crossed her mind. She thought how well he looked in his dark coat and white breeches, how much strength of character showed in the set of his shoulders and that firm chin. Their eyes met briefly, and she turned away to make some trifling remark to Lady Warham, who was sitting beside her on the sofa. She did not intend him to think she had been waiting for him to appear.

Lady Warham unconsciously made matters more difficult for her by rising with a whispered, "You will wish to sit by your husband," and going to another chair. But before Wynford could take advantage of this move — if, indeed, he had meant to do so — Ralph Melbury slipped quickly into the vacant place.

"Your husband must be prepared to share you sometimes," he said, smiling. "One man cannot be permitted to keep so much charm entirely to himself."

"You are very good, sir. And I think he may easily feel he has the best of the bargain, for he's talking to your wife," countered Emma.

"Ah, so he is. You met Kitty at Tiffany's, in Weymouth, as I understand?"

"Yes. It was a fortunate thing for me, as we were but lately arrived, and didn't know anyone — or, at least, scarcely anyone," she amended.

"Then you do have some acquaintance in the neighbourhood?"

"My husband does — some Army officers."

"I think I had heard that he was once a military man. Does he not miss the life?"

Emma hesitated, uncertain how to answer this. "I don't think so — at least, he never gives me to understand that he does," she said, at last, forcing a smile.

"Ah, no, naturally not. With so charming a companion, what man could be churlish enough to suggest that he might prefer to be elsewhere? But in the present state of affairs, you know, ma'am, with an invasion from the Continent daily expected on every hand, it would scarcely be surprising if he took it into his head to return."

She felt that he was watching her very closely as he said this, and she became uneasy. Had she said anything to give him cause for suspicion?

"Well," she replied, brazening it out, "if he does feel like that, he says nothing of it to me. And I do beg you, sir —" she thought that this was an artistic touch — "not to suggest anything of the kind to him! The thought of it near distracts me!"

"Oh, no, no — have no fear," he said, soothingly. "I shall say nothing. And it is only while you remain near the coast that you will hear invasion talk. I dare say in London there is not so much said about it. You did come from London, I believe?"

Emma answered that they did and tried hard to think of a change of subject.

"I don't go there myself, nowadays, but once I knew it well. Whereabouts is your home, when you are in Town?"

"We have a house in Albemarle Street." She knew that Wynford had one there, and this was what they had agreed to say. All the same, her uneasiness was increasing; so far, no one had questioned her so closely about the period before the supposed Wynfords came to Dorset.

He nodded approvingly. "A most convenient situation. I have some friends who live in that very street — at No. 37. The name is Pletherington. Possibly you may know them?"

Emma carefully schooled her face to show no expression, but her fingers tightened on the reticule she was holding. "I fear we don't — but in London one isn't so fortunate as in the country, where one may soon become acquainted with one's neighbours," she answered, smiling.

"Just so." His voice was smooth. "But there are other advantages, which my wife will certainly tell you she would envy you — parties, and balls, Ranelagh and Almack's — do you take part in all these diversions, ma'am?"

Emma inclined her head, still smiling. "But not very recently," she said. "You may perhaps know, Mr. Melbury, that my health has not been good of late."

"And for that reason, Mrs. Wynford, we are privileged to have you among us at present. But why did you not try Brighton? It is nearer to town and is just as salubrious as Weymouth. And I believe — correct me if I err — that you are familiar with the resort, as you were staying there when you first met your husband."

Emma's lips felt dry, but her smile never wavered. She looked away from Ralph Melbury, catching Wynford's eye for a second. It was long enough; he detached himself from the group where he was standing and sauntered over to the sofa.

"Yes, that is so," she agreed. "But Brighton is more bracing, and the doctor thought perhaps a softer air —" She broke off as Wynford reached them. "Mr. Melbury was just asking me why we chose Weymouth rather than Brighton," she greeted him. "Perhaps you will tell him all about it, for I must have a word with Mrs. Melbury for a moment."

She went over to Kitty and chatted to her with a good deal of animation for a few moments, before making her way to the room which had been made over to the use of the lady visitors. There was a housemaid in attendance, so Emma had to keep up an appearance of having retired there for the usual reasons; but her real object had been to escape for a while in order to recover her poise. This had been badly shaken by Mr. Melbury's persistent questioning, but she hoped that she had managed to conceal the fact.

She had been there only a few moments when Lady Warham walked into the room.

"Oh, there you are, my dear. I wondered if perhaps you did not feel well," she said, solicitously.

"No, thank you, ma'am, I am perfectly all right," replied Emma, making some pretence of patting her hair into place before the mirror. "Still, it was kind in you."

"Not at all. Meeting new people can be tiring, I know, especially when one is recovering from an illness. You mustn't allow your strength to be overtaxed. Should you wish to leave early, I will make the first move, if you like. It will perhaps come better from me as an established acquaintance of the Melburys."

Emma thanked her again. "Has Mr. Melbury lived in this neighbourhood for a long time, ma'am?" she added.

"Oh, yes. He inherited the house from a relative — let me see, it must be more than ten years ago — but he was living in London at that time with his former wife and did not come into Dorset very frequently. Then about six years back, he sold up the London house, and has lived here ever since. His first wife died a few years afterwards, and after an interval he married Kitty." She dropped her voice. "We wondered if it would answer at first — she was so young, and so far away from her relatives and former friends. But she spends a good deal of time in visits to them, though I notice they never come here. And, of course, Mr. Melbury has always kept open house to the neighbourhood — he is most hospitable. All the same, I sometimes wonder —" She broke off, and laughed in a half-ashamed manner. "I have a daughter of Kitty Melbury's age — and of yours, too, my dear — and as all my children are married and living some distance from us, I fear I have a regrettable tendency to exercise my maternal instinct on my neighbours! You must forgive me."

"For my part, I am grateful for such benevolent interest," replied Emma, sincerely. "My own mother died when I was very young."

Lady Warham made no reply but looked at her compassionately as they both returned to the drawing room, where Kitty Melbury was busy pouring out tea for her guests. She handed a cup to her husband, but he refused it with a wave of the hand.

"Did you not hear me say I didn't wish for tea?" he asked her. Emma thought it was said rather sharply.

Kitty looked startled, and placed the cup on the table hastily, so that some of the liquid slopped into the saucer. He said nothing, but frowned with a quelling look, then signalled to the housemaid to take the cup away.

Emma glanced quickly at Wynford and saw that he, too, was watching. He came towards her and settled her in a chair close to where Captain and Mrs. Rivers were seated.

"By the way, Wynford, did you see the Dorchester Journal today?" asked Captain, Rivers. "Shocking thing, that corpse they found in the old castle ruins, what?"

"Corpse?" repeated his wife, Jane, with a shudder. "Really, Geoffrey, I do think that's scarcely a topic for the drawing room!"

"Sorry, m'dear." The fact was that Captain Rivers had partaken freely enough of his host's wine to forget for the moment that there were ladies present. "Deuced odd thing, though. Did you see it, Shirley?"

Thomas Shirley shook his head a shade repressively.

"Oh, pray, do tell us all about it!" gushed Charlotte Shirley. "It sounds prodigiously Gothic — just like Mrs. Radcliffe, you know!"

Captain Rivers smiled at her in a foolish way and proceeded to ignore his wife's continued protests.

"Well, it seems a few days ago someone found this corpse hidden away in the ruins — man was murdered — stabbed. Nothing on him to say who he was, but the Journal suggests he may have been a French spy. Don't know about that, myself — more likely a pickpocket who got his deserts, what? Still, odd thing that someone took the trouble to hide the body away. Suppose we shall never know the truth of it."

"A French spy!" breathed Charlotte Shirley. "Oh, do you really think, Mr. Melbury, that there can be any spies in this neighbourhood? I declare, the mere supposition quite sends shivers down my spine!"

"And mine, too!" Mrs. Rivers was visibly trembling a little with fright. "Really, Geoffrey, it's a great deal too bad of you to repeat such a tale, just when we were all so comfortable together! And now I feel I cannot be easy until I get home to my children — Heaven knows what might happen to them, if this should prove true!"

"True enough," repeated her husband, obstinately. "The corpse, I mean. Don't know about the rest."

"All a hum, I should say," scoffed Sir Edward Warham, leaning over to pat his wife's hand reassuringly, although she was showing no sign whatever of alarm. "These journalist chaps, *I* know, always out to put sensation into everything. Shouldn't wonder if Rivers hadn't hit on the true explanation — some felon or other who would have ended on the gallows, anyway."

Emma was watching Wynford. He had made no contribution to the foregoing conversation but had sat there sipping his tea and seeming to be only half attending. At the first mention of a body in the castle ruins, she had found difficulty in repressing a start, for her mind had jumped at once to what she had overheard that first night at Poyntz Manor. As she studied him speculatively, she tried to recall the exact words. There had been something said about some connection being found between him and the dead man. What if it should be true that the murdered man had been a French spy? In spite of what Sir Edward said, those responsible for writing the newspapers often did hit on the truth. That would mean — she caught her breath suddenly on the thought — that Rupert Wynford was also engaged in espionage for the French.

It would explain so much. The carefully planned masquerade which would serve as a cover for his real activities; the detailed knowledge he possessed of their neighbours, although he had never met them before; his readiness to mix with them socially, and his insistence that Emma should pass on to him any further information about them which she might acquire.

Why this particular area and the people living there? But surely Wynford himself had given her the answer to that. If an invasion should come, Dorset was one of the most likely places for attack. The knowledge of military matters which she had gleaned from her father told her the rest. A French agent would seek to discover all he could of the area's defence measures and those who were to implement them. His mission would be to prepare the way for an invading force. Doubtless there would be others doing the same work in various parts of the country vulnerable to attack; but here in Dorset Rupert Wynford was the man.

Suddenly she felt certain of it, and a sick feeling swept over her.

What ought she to do?

THIRTEEN

A restless night failed to supply the answer; and when Matilda came in with the hot water at a little after nine o'clock, Emma felt heavy-eyed and dispirited. Matilda, however, was bursting with vitality.

"Oh, ma'am!" she exclaimed. "Such excitement down to Preston as you'd never believe! The King and Queen and the Princesses, God bless 'em, all in carriages, passed through on their way to Weymouth not an hour agone! And all the redcoats riding beside them, and the villagers turning out to cheer — as brave a sight as never was, so says Betty and Jem, who was lucky enough to be there to see it all!"

"Yes, I'm sure it was," replied Emma, forcing a smile. "What time is it, Matilda?"

"Past nine, ma'am. I did look in earlier, but you was so sound asleep, it seemed a shame to disturb you. But Master left a message to say he'd be back just after ten to go with you to Osmington, so I thought I'd best rouse you now."

"To Osmington?" Emma's tired brain did not take in the significance of this, at first, and then she remembered that they had been invited to visit the Warhams at Osmington Manor today. "Oh, yes, of course. In that case, please put out my riding dress, Matilda, for Mr. Wynford mentioned that we should ride there if the weather permitted." She looked towards the window with its view of sunlit green hills. "It seems fine enough. Did Mr. Wynford go out early?"

"About six, ma'am, just as the household was stirring," replied the abigail, emptying some water from the ewer into a basin decorated with rosebuds, and adding a dash of some fragrance from a glass bottle. "Gentlemen like a deal of exercise, don't they, ma'am? Master goes off riding most mornings."

Emma assented, but privately she wondered for the first time what really did lie behind Wynford's early morning absences. Previously she, too, had supposed that he liked the exercise. Was it in fact something more sinister?

She was crossing the hall on her way to the morning parlour when he came into the house, handing his gloves and whip to a servant. He smiled at her as though their altercation of the previous evening had never happened.

"Are you about to breakfast, my love? Then I'll join you, if I may, for I went out fasting. A moment, only, while I freshen up a trifle."

He took the stairs two at a time and vanished in the direction of his bedchamber. Emma continued into the parlour, where breakfast was set out for her, and desired another place to be laid. In a few minutes he joined her and began inflicting severe punishment on the plate of ham which was placed before him. Presently he looked up.

"You look charming, Emma," he said, approvingly. "Russet brings out the golden tints in your hair."

She thanked him coyly, for the benefit of the servant who was waiting on them; but her heart hardened at the thought of the last compliment he had paid her, and his subsequent behaviour. He appeared to follow her thoughts, for he smiled cynically.

Soon they were both mounted and riding along the bridleway which led across country to Osmington. She was silent; there seemed nothing that she could say to him, so she gave herself up to the simple pleasure of movement through green meadows beside gentle hill slopes under a blue sky touched with soft white cloud.

"I see you are still vexed with me," he said, after a while.

"Why should you think so?" Her tone was not encouraging.

"Because I'm beginning to know you, Emma. But come — I'm not the man to keep up a quarrel. If I beg your pardon for what happened the other evening, will you forgive me?"

"It is my plain duty to do so, is it not?"

He wrinkled his nose in disgust. "Not like that. Say we can be friends once more."

"I think something more is needed before I can say that," she replied, distantly.

"Something more?" He studied her for a moment, then nodded. "I think you mean that you require an assurance that it will not happen again."

"Precisely."

"Well, I can't give it — not with certainty. What I will promise is to do my best. Word of a gentleman. There, will that satisfy you? And here's my hand on it."

Taking the reins in his left hand, he leaned over in the saddle to offer her his right. Her horse, a gentle enough animal, but a little nervous, shied slightly at the sudden movement. At once his hand came down firmly over hers, controlling the rein.

"I assure you I am quite capable of managing the mare," she said, with dignity.

"And everything else," he replied, removing his hand. "Deuce take it, Emma, you don't understand! You are so — and I — oh, hell and the devil! There's so much I would like to say to you — was ever man in such a devil of a coil!"

"Well, it's your own fault if you are," she retorted. "The tangle's of your own making, after all. Why don't you tell me the meaning of this extraordinary masquerade, if you really wish me to understand your situation?"

They were riding abreast, the horses slowed to a walking pace. Rupert Wynford turned his face towards her as she spoke; for a moment she read indecision there and knew that she was within a short step of learning his secret.

The sound of hoofs thudding over the turf close behind them made Wynford turn sharply, to see a uniformed rider approaching. As the gentleman drew nearer, he shouted a cheerful greeting, and they realised it was Lieutenant Tilley. Emma noticed that Wynford made an instinctive movement of impatience; but he answered the other man amiably enough. Lieutenant Tilley bowed to Emma as he reined in his horse.

"A fine morning," he said, smiling. "Where are you bound? Anywhere in particular?"

Wynford replied that they were riding over to Osmington Manor to call on the Warhams.

"Capital! I am going that way. May I ride with you?"

Wynford's permission sounded ready enough, but Emma saw by the expression in his eyes that he was not best pleased. She reflected with some surprise that she must be coming to know him rather too well, since she was now able to interpret some of his looks. But this was only to be expected when one lived at close quarters to another person: and it did not help at all in solving the mystery which surrounded them.

Lieutenant Tilley kept up a ready flow of light conversation, addressing himself as often to Emma as to Wynford, and managing to ride beside her for most of the time. She found herself responding easily to his lead, and as they laughed together the weight lifted from her spirits.

At length they joined a lane which ran past the drive to Osmington Manor and continued into the village itself. They pulled up outside the Manor gates and Lieutenant Tilley took his leave.

"You must call on us sometime," said Emma, spontaneously, as she said goodbye.

"With the greatest pleasure in the world, ma'am," he replied promptly, bowing. "To our next meeting, then. Servant, Wynford."

"Young coxcomb," muttered Wynford, as they rode down the avenue of beeches. "What on earth did you want to invite him for?"

"Because I understood that you wished to become acquainted with everyone in the neighbourhood," she replied, good-humouredly.

"I'm already as much acquainted with him as I desire to be." His tone was acid. "He's a distant cousin of Gill's and I met him when Juliana and I first came down here to reconnoitre — I thought I'd told you this before."

"So you did, but I'd forgotten," she said, airily. "Anyway, I like him."

"That is evident."

They had reached the door of the Manor by this time, so Emma was spared the necessity of replying. They were admitted by a staid butler into a pleasant parlour at the back of the house, overlooking a sunken garden with a fountain playing in its centre. After they had taken some refreshment, Sir Edward Warham took Wynford off to the stables to inspect his horses, while Emma and Lady Warham remained in the parlour, enjoying a relaxed conversation which placed no great intellectual strain on either.

Lady Warham had been speaking of her married daughters and their offspring with the interest natural to one of her maternal nature, when she broke off suddenly, saying contritely

— "But there, perhaps I should not prose so on that subject. But if you will not think it impertinent of me, my dear Mrs. Wynford, may I reassure you? A miscarriage is unfortunate, of course; but it does not mean quite the end of one's hopes, when one is as young and naturally robust as I believe you to be. Never fear, in time you will produce a fine, stout baby such as will delight both your hearts."

Emma could not help herself; she blushed a fiery red. Lady Warham patted her hand.

"There, I beg your pardon! I have embarrassed you by speaking of it. Forgive me, my dear, but we are quite alone, and I am old enough to be your mother — indeed, my own daughters are older than you."

Emma shook her head. "No, not at all — it's just that I'm stupid — and you are all kindness, ma'am."

They could say no more on that subject, as the two gentlemen returned to the room, and the conversation became general.

Later, as they were riding back, Wynford asked curiously. "What did Lady Warham have to say to you that made you blush so rosily? Never was so much colour in the sunset!"

"Oh, it was all my foolishness," answered Emma, evasively, turning her head away to scan the hillside.

"What kind of foolishness?" he persisted.

"Must you know everything? There are some matters which should be private between females."

He flashed a keen look at her. "Then I think I can hazard a guess. There seems to be a general notion prevailing in the neighbourhood that your supposed recent indisposition was — hm! — of an order to be anticipated among married ladies. It's natural that they should think this, and useful, too, from our point of view, for it serves to corroborate our story."

She said nothing but looked scornful.

"I must remind you," he said sharply, "that we have a contract, you and I. I don't wish to be brutal, but I expect you to do your utmost to fulfil it. You yourself say that you consider your remuneration adequate, but if you have had second thoughts about that —"

"Money!" She threw the word at him contemptuously. "There are things of greater importance — honour, fair dealing, peace of mind. They are all lost to me since I started on this wicked masquerade!"

"Wicked?" His tone was strange.

"Yes, wicked! You are practising a deception on respectable, worthy people — when I think of Lady Warham, so kind, so gentle, I hate myself for taking her in so shamefully! Could she but know the truth, what would she think of me? And for what purpose are we living this lie? It cannot be anything but a wicked one!"

"Sometimes a small evil is necessary to serve a greater good," he replied, soberly.

"Fustian! You are full of excuses; but if you were not ashamed of your purpose, you would confide it to me."

He was silent for a few moments. She wondered if at last he was about to confide in her. And with this thought came the sudden realisation that she was hoping against hope that he could produce some explanation which would show him in a favourable light, which would totally dispel her growing suspicion that he was a spy for the French.

"There might be another reason for keeping you in ignorance," he said at last. "Sometimes knowledge is dangerous." The deep seriousness of his tone made her shiver, and she knew now that he would tell her nothing. "Speak of this no more!" he commanded, brusquely. "Tell me instead what I have been meaning to ask you before — what Melbury was saying to you yesterday evening."

She silently swallowed her disappointment. "He was asking a great many questions. He wanted to know if you did not miss your former military life, and whether you ever spoke of returning to it."

He raised his eyebrows. "So he has heard of my military past? Well, I haven't tried to keep that any particular secret — one must have some origins, after all, and the Army is harmless enough."

She nodded. "It was part of the story we agreed to tell. But what I found more disturbing was his curiosity about our previous life in London. I told him we had a house in Albemarle Street and he asked if we were acquainted with some people whom he knows there, named — I think it was Pletherington. I must confess that did shake my confidence somewhat, for I was not sure how far the story I was telling was based on the truth."

"The most convincing stories always have a basis of fact," he replied, imperturbably. "Yes, I actually do have a house there, though I spend very little time in it, and consequently know few of the other residents. What did you say to him?"

"That it wasn't as easy to know one's neighbours in London as it is in the country. It was the only thing I could think of at the time."

"You couldn't have done better," he approved. "Well done, Emma — your stage training stood you in good stead there. Was that all the conversation?"

"No. He went on to ask about London diversions and I feared that he might catch me out on some such matter as what plays had been performed at such-and-such a time, and so on. So I told him I hadn't taken part in many outings of late, owing to indifferent health. You know the rest, for I had to ask you to give an answer when he began to question me about Brighton."

"Yes," he said, thoughtfully. "His information about me was as complete as it well could be, wasn't it? Only Captain Gill knows that we were supposed to have met in Brighton — it hasn't been necessary to divulge that part of our story to anyone else, so far. Odd — I wonder if he's acquainted with Gill. He may well be, as they're both members of the Club in St. Mary Street. Hm! It seems Ralph Melbury will bear watching."

He lapsed into silence for some time. Emma studied his face, reading in it signs of one wrestling with a problem. She wished she knew what it was about.

"Well," he said, at last coming out of his reverie. "No doubt you'll have learnt that the Royal Family arrived today. Tomorrow being Sunday, they will have their day of rest, and we must show ourselves in Church, I suppose. But if it continues fine on Monday would you like to go into Weymouth and see them take their morning dip? As I warned you before, you must rise early to do so, for Farmer George is no sluggard!"

FOURTEEN

By six o'clock in the morning, the Esplanade was crowded. Military red and navy blue mingled with fresh muslins and gay bonnets, with top hats and coats of superfine. Bathing machines were drawn up on the beach with brawny "dippers", both male and female, in attendance. Not far from these, a large crowd of the humbler Weymouth residents stood by to watch their King enter the water.

A cheer rose suddenly in every throat, as from one of the machines stepped a man divested of every adornment to indicate his Royalty. As he was plunged into the sea by attentive dippers, a brass band from a neighbouring machine struck up the strains of "God Save Great George our King."

"And will you follow?" asked Wynford of Emma, as he held tightly on to her arm for fear they should become separated in the crowd.

She laughed. "Oh, I think not quite at once. It would be almost lese majeste, would it not? But later, perhaps, I might venture to try. The sea is so very gentle here — not as boisterous as it is at Brighton."

"So you do know Brighton, after all?" he said, in a low tone.

"I was there once with my father."

"Your father? Was he also on the stage?"

She shook her head, but volunteered nothing more, and he did not press her.

"Let us try and make our way into the town," he said, when they had been standing there for some time and had looked their fill. "There is a tolerable inn, where perhaps we can get some refreshment."

They made their way through the crowds with some difficulty, and at one stage he placed an arm about her to protect her from the worst of the buffeting. She was conscious of his nearness but had to admit to herself that he was making no attempt to turn the protective gesture into an embrace. He released her as soon as they had negotiated the thickest part of the crowd, placing her hand upon his arm again in a commendably decorous manner.

They turned into one of the streets leading off the Esplanade, and had gone some way along it when, hearing his name called, Wynford turned to see Captain Gill on the opposite pavement, accompanied by his wife and Lieutenant Tilley. The three crossed over to join them, and by common consent continued with them to the inn, where they succeeded in commandeering a private parlour.

As usual, Mrs. Gill was not particularly talkative; and as her husband more or less monopolized Rupert Wynford at first, it was left to Tilley to entertain Emma. This he did so successfully that she was soon laughing. Wynford glanced at her once with a flash of his dark eyes, but otherwise continued his conversation with Gill.

"I thought you told me," said Emma severely, "that you had very important work to do at your signal station, yet you always seem to be gadding about here, there and everywhere! It will not do, sir."

"Oh, well, Mrs. Wynford, a fellow must have some respite. All work and no play, you know, what? Besides, I've been given a few days furlough just at present. Too much of interest going on for me to stay perched up on a hill, away from it all. There are things — and people —" he looked at her significantly — "I wouldn't miss for the world."

"Such as seeing His Majesty take a bathe?"

"That, of course. And such as enjoying the company of two so charming ladies —" with a bow in Mrs. Gill's direction.

"Oh, you're very ready with your compliments, sir!" laughed Emma. "But Mrs. Gill and I are not to be taken in, are we, ma'am? We know that you say this kind of thing to all the females you meet."

"If he does not," said Mrs. Gill, with a smile, making one of her rare contributions to the conversation, "he is unlike most of the other young officers in my husband's regiment."

"Well, perhaps I do now and then," conceded Tilley, his eyes twinkling. "But only in the way of civility, you understand. I never mean the compliment sincerely, as I do at present."

Emma turned a helpless look in Mrs. Gill's direction. "You see, ma'am, he is quite incorrigible. What shall we do with him?"

Mrs. Gill only shook her head in answer to this; and before the light-hearted verbal sparring could begin afresh, Captain Gill and Wynford had joined in the conversation.

Presently, Gill mentioned that there was to be a review of the troops by His Majesty on Bincombe Down on the following day.

"You'll be there, Wynford, I suppose? And Mrs. Wynford, if she feels up to it, what?"

Wynford looked enquiringly at Emma. She nodded. "Oh, yes, I should like it extremely."

"I shall be there in the way of duty, of course," continued Gill. "Tilley here is to escort my wife, and there'll be one or two other officers' ladies in the party. Why don't you and Mrs. Wynford join 'em, what? Shame to leave Charlie without another man in the party — not but what he might prefer it, eh, Charles? Must warn you, ma'am —" here he leaned towards Emma, pretending to lower his voice — "he's a bit of a lady-killer, by all accounts. Good thing we're related, y'know, or he might call me out for that," he added, grinning.

"Call you out, Maurice?" asked Tilley, in mock horror. "I hope I have more sense of self preservation. I understand you're a devilish good shot."

"Bah, don't think to take me in with your flattery — keep it for the females, m'boy! But what d'you say, Wynford? Does it suit you to join them?"

Put like that, it was difficult for Rupert Wynford to refuse, although Emma fancied that she saw a hint of reluctance in his expression. There was no doubt about it, she could sometimes tell what was passing through his mind; she could only wish that all his thoughts might be as clear to her.

She was less sure of her powers of perception the next morning, when she heard him inviting Captain and Mrs. Gill and Lieutenant Tilley to dine at Poyntz Manor after the review was over. He had previously issued an invitation for that evening to the party they had met at the Melburys' house, and all but the Reverend and Mrs. Bredy had agreed to come. They had pleaded a prior engagement, for which Emma had felt profoundly thankful. She had rarely taken such an instant dislike as she had done to the elegant Mrs. Bredy. But since Rupert Wynford was evidently willing to include the present company in that invitation, she must have been wrong in supposing that he had wished to avoid them.

He was silent on the journey back to Poytnz Manor and left her to herself for the rest of the day. Having consulted Mrs. Hinton about the extra guests for tomorrow evening, she spent the time before dinner in reading "The Vicar of Wakefield," which had been a favourite novel of her father's; and in working on an embroidered cushion cover which was intended for her old schoolmistress in Cumberland whom she meant to visit when this wretched business in Dorset was at an end. She would have enough money then for the journey, and perhaps Miss Bartlett would be able to help her to find a post as a governess or companion in that area. A personal recommendation from an established resident of good character might possibly compensate for the lack of a more formal reference. Juliana Hythe had said that some arrangements would be made for her after her term with Mr. Wynford was at an end; but she had no intention of waiting to see what these arrangements might be. Apart from the fact that they would be based on the false assumption that she was an actress, her pride revolted at the notion of allowing him to have any hand in her future. She wished never to see or even to think of him again once she had left Poyntz Ferrers. At this point in her reflections, she jabbed incautiously at the material with her needle and caught her finger, raising a pinprick of blood.

Little was said at dinner beyond a discussion of arrangements for the following day. After he had joined her in the drawing room and the servants had been dismissed, he stood leaning against the mantlepiece looking down at her in what she found a slightly unnerving way. She gave no sign, however, sitting with hands gently clasped in her lap.

He cleared his throat, and she looked up at him.

"This fellow Tilley," he said, abruptly. "I have wondered —" He stopped. She raised her eyebrows inquiringly. "What do you really think of him?" he continued, studying her face.

"Oh, I don't know," she answered, carelessly. Then, as she saw he continued to watch her expression closely, she added perversely — "He's a very charming gentleman, of course, and most agreeable company."

"Is that all, Emma?"

"All? Why, what can you mean, Mr. Wynford?"

"I had wondered," he said, slowly, "if you were developing — a tendre for him."

A faint blush appeared on her cheek. She shook her head without speaking.

"Hm," he said, with a twist of the lips. "Well, if you are, Emma, it puts us in the devil of a coil. As far as he knows, you are my wife."

"You can scarcely suppose me to have forgotten that!"

"Perhaps not — but one's emotions are not always subject to control." She fancied there was a certain bitterness in his tone. "I must warn you, Emma, that there can be no happy ending to such a love affair. Tilley thinks you a married woman, therefore he is only flirting. As for you —" He broke off, turned away, and took a few hasty strides round the room. At last he swung round to face her. "You must get over it, Emma. I'm sorry — deeply sorry —" his voice faltered a little, then gathered strength — "but there's nothing else for it. There is more involved in this than you realise. In short, one's personal feelings must be set aside. Possibly things may not have gone too far for you to make a recovery. With all my heart, I hope it may prove so."

Before she could answer, he had flung himself out of the room.

She scarcely knew what to think. His tone had held more of sorrow than anger, although he was the kind of man to show annoyance at any hitch in his carefully laid schemes. It seemed he pitied her — how absurd! She was in no danger of losing her head over the charming Lieutenant, agreeable though she might find his light-hearted attentions. Then why had she tried to make Rupert Wynford think otherwise? She smiled; he could not expect to have things all his own way. A feeling of gentle tolerance towards him crept over her.

It lasted until she was ready to climb into bed after Matilda had left her. The last thing she always did at this time was to make quite sure that the door communicating with Wynford's bedchamber was shut. She had come to the conclusion that the servants must use it as a short cut when cleaning the rooms, as she had frequently found it left ajar after that first night. She had never locked it, in spite of the key he had provided; deciding that there was too much danger that she might forget to unlock it again before Matilda came to her in the mornings. Tonight, as often, it was not quite closed. She was about to shut it firmly when she heard a slight movement in the room beyond. She drew back, then retreated towards her bed. She climbed in and blew out the candle, telling herself that she would get out later and shut it by the wavering light of the moon which shone in through the windows from which Matilda, at her request, had drawn back the curtains. Her intentions came to nothing, for she fell asleep almost immediately.

She was awakened by a sound which she could not at first identify. She pushed herself up a little on the pillows, listening. Hailstones? Could there be hail in late August, and with the weather still so perfect? Then she realised that the sound had been cut off too abruptly for any kind of natural shower. Someone must have thrown a handful of small stones or dirt against the window; a trick which her father had employed on one occasion, she recalled suddenly, when he had forgotten his key.

Thoroughly awake now, she darted from the bed to the window and peered through the casement, which was slightly ajar to admit the night air which Matilda was convinced was injurious to her mistress's health. But the aperture was not wide enough for her to see anything underneath the window, even if the moon had not at that moment chanced to be overcast.

She hesitated, wondering whether to open the casement fully and put out her head. Could Wynford have forgotten his key, like her father, returning to find all the servants abed? Even as she hesitated, she heard sounds of cautious movement from the adjoining room. Evidently Burton had heard the summons and would go to the rescue. There was nothing for her to do but return to bed.

She delayed a moment or two longer, then moved slowly over towards the communicating door, with some thought of trying to hear if Rupert Wynford did succeed in reaching his room. Presently her straining ears caught the sound of the door to his bedchamber closing softly, and then the murmur of voices. She was about to turn away, satisfied, when she realised that the voices which came faintly to her ears were not only the familiar ones of Wynford and his valet, but also of two men who were strangers to her.

Her heart began to beat faster. This was obviously a secret meeting, and in view of what she already suspected about Rupert Wynford, it was her plain duty to try and overhear what was passing. It was not going to be easy. The four men were speaking in low tones, and she knew from previous experience that they could only be heard at all clearly when they chanced to be standing close to the door. It was not a large room, however, and if she could manage to ease the door open a little farther —

She took a deep breath. It might prove a dangerous enterprise. Supposing she should be discovered, what could she say? She began to rehearse to herself some kind of defence, at the same time realising on another level of consciousness that all this was indeed turning her into an actress. She thought of Bonaparte's invading army, stealing to England's sleeping shores at the dark of the moon, helped by these men. Her resolve hardened. Her father had left no son behind to serve his country, but perhaps a daughter might do something to prove herself worthy of her father's memory.

She put out an unsteady hand and eased the door forward an inch or so.

Nothing happened. Encouraged, she leaned forward to peer through the narrow crack into the room beyond. She realised at once that it was too dimly lit for the movement of the door to have been noticed unless one of the occupants had been looking that way at the same time. She could see part of the shoulder of one of them turned away from her and guessed that they were all earnestly engaged in conversation. She set herself to listen.

At first, she could only glean meaningless fragments. A reference to highwaymen seemed to cause some quickly suppressed amusement; and at one stage she gained the impression that Wynford was issuing orders to the others. But nothing came to her clearly until she detected some movement within her range of vision. Evidently, Wynford had come closer to the door, for she could now detect most of what he was saying, as she was familiar with his voice.

"Several possibilities — Rivers of Preston's a gamester: I hear he's up to his ears in debt. Then there's Shirley at Bincombe. Keen on farming, spends a deal on modern improvements —" here she lost the thread for a moment, until another familiar name caught her ear. "Warham — still working on that, but nothing as far as I know, except that he's a member of the gaming club. As for the Reverend Bredy, he has a very expensive wife. Any of 'em could be open to subversion. Then there's Melbury."

The speaker broke off here, and one of the others put in a remark which Emma failed to catch.

"Yes, well," continued Wynford, "asked the girl a good many questions. He's a sociable man, so it could have been idle curiosity about neighbours. On the other hand, might suspect something. If so, he could be the one Abney was looking for."

Somebody else made a reference to this name, which Emma realised was that of the man who had been found murdered in the castle ruins, whom Mr. Rivers had said was thought to be a spy for the French.

"We shall never know now, more's the pity," answered Wynford. "He did put us on to Tiffany, though, and she's a valuable link. Now that my supposed wife's a client there, matters should be —" His voice broke off abruptly. There was a sudden movement within her narrow range of vision, and all at once the door was jerked roughly open.

She stood face to face with Wynford, who stood staring at her incredulously for a moment.

"Emma!" His voice rose to its natural tone on the word. The next moment, it sank to a furious whisper. "What the devil are you doing?"

She heard muttered exclamations from the other men, and one of them seized a candlestick and brought it over to the door. Its light showed Wynford's face grim, his dark eyes glittering. She stood there, shrinking, as pale as a ghost in her white nightgown; but she remembered the rehearsed excuse.

"I — I was awakened by voices from your room, and I realised the maids must have left this door open again — so — so — I came to shut it," she stammered.

He seized her roughly by the wrist and dragged her forward into his bedchamber. "How long have you been there?" he demanded harshly. "How much of our talk have you heard?"

"I — only a minute or so —"

He gave her imprisoned arm a little shake. "Don't try to gammon me, Emma! I warn you, you'll catch cold at that!"

She drew herself up with what dignity she could muster, although her teeth were chattering. She clenched them fiercely.

"Kindly let me go!" she managed to say at last. "I have not the — smallest interest in — in what *gentlemen* —" she gave a scornful inflection to the word — "choose to say to each other in their cups. Neither do I care to — to be exhibited in this fashion before —" she gave a quick glance round the room — "your servant and two total strangers."

He gave a sign to the others. Then, snatching the candlestick from the man who was holding it, he pushed her before him into her own room, closing the door behind them. Only then did he release her.

He held the candle so that its light shone on to her grey eyes, wide with fear, and her dead white cheeks.

"Now tell me the truth!" he grated.

She was terrified now but clung desperately to her story. "I — I have told you already. If you don't choose to believe me, I can't help it," she said, weakly. "Please — please permit me to go back to bed, I implore you."

He stood quite still, staring at her as though he would try and read the truth from her expression.

She could think of only one defence, and put up her hands to her head, swaying a little as though about to faint. He set down the candlestick with an oath and put his arms about her.

"For God's sake, Emma, don't swoon!" he muttered, in a tone of near panic. "I can't summon your abigail just now, and

I'm no hand at the business! Devil take it, girl, bear up a little, can't you?"

He raised his hand and gently smoothed her hair back from her face. Somehow or other, her own hands had come to rest on his shoulders. He tilted her chin a little, looked long into her eyes and then bent his head as if to kiss her.

Just in time, she gave him a little push and straightened up.

"I'm all right now," she said, in a constrained tone. "Pray leave me alone — goodnight."

He watched her move towards the bed; then, taking up the candle, he went from the room.

FIFTEEN

At any other time, Emma would have enjoyed the Military Review on Bincombe Down. Coaches, curricles, phaetons and gigs thronged every approach road for hours before the time appointed, creating a holiday feeling in spite of the inevitable irritations of traffic congestion. And the spectacle of that imposing array of scarlet uniforms drawn up in symmetrical lines on the green saucer of the Down, which was fringed with the ancient burial grounds of much earlier warriors, could scarcely fail to quicken the imagination of anyone with military connections.

But although her eyes were pleased by the picture before her, her mind was too uneasy for her to make a very lively member of their party; and presently Lieutenant Tilley taxed her with this, asking why she was not in spirits today.

"Am I not?" she replied, attempting to laugh. "I think perhaps I am a trifle overawed by so much pomp and panoply."

"Oh, think nothing of it, ma'am. We must show the flag a trifle, now and then, y'know; but beneath those scarlet tunics beat hearts which would stand far more in awe of lovely ladies like yourself," he countered, promptly.

She returned some light answer to this, and afterwards tried to take a more active part in the conversation, thinking ruefully that she was well on the way to becoming the actress she was thought to be.

Once the Review was over, the party dispersed, Wynford giving a reminder to those members of it who were to dine at Poyntz Manor later in the day. Nothing was said about the events of the previous evening on the short journey back to the Manor; and, as she was now coming to expect, Wynford left Emma to herself for the rest of the day. She was greeted by Matilda with enthusiasm, as Madame Tiffany had delivered the clothes which had been ordered.

"Oh, do pray come and look, ma'am!" urged the girl, excitedly. "There's all manner of pretty gowns and I know not what! I've unpacked them and laid some out on the bed for you to try on, and hung up the rest for the time being —"

Emma smiled at her eagerness but shook her head. "Perhaps I will, later; but truth to tell, I'm so weary now, Matilda, that I had thought I might lie down for a while. I didn't sleep well last night, and there's to be company in the house this evening."

Matilda, instantly full of compassion, said that she would put the garments away for the present, and darted upstairs ahead of her mistress to perform the task. She had almost completed it when Emma finally arrived in her bedchamber, having stopped on the way to have a few words with Mrs. Hinton. Only two gowns still remained carefully draped on the bed; one was a day dress of pink spotted muslin, the other a more elaborate evening gown in a soft shade of yellow, with a train.

Emma gazed at them in delight, her weariness receding. "Perhaps I will just try on these two," she said, yielding to a very feminine impulse. "If I mean to lie down for a while, I'll be obliged to remove the gown I am wearing, in any case."

Matilda, only too ready to comply with this, helped her mistress out of her gown and, following Emma's directions, into the pink muslin.

"Oh!" breathed Matilda, in rapture. "Oh, Mrs. Wynford, ma'am, it do become you!"

Emma nodded in satisfaction, noticing how the pink shade added a soft glow to her cheeks, which were a little paler than usual this morning. "Yes, I believe it does." She twisted round before the long mirror. "It's a good fit, but I fancy — don't you? — that the skirt doesn't hang quite as it should at this one side. Can you see?"

Matilda stooped down so that her eyes were more on the level of the skirt and requested her mistress to turn round slowly. This Emma did several times, until she suddenly lost patience with the exercise, her tiredness returning.

"Let us leave it to Madame Tiffany — she'll know at once where it's at fault. You may hang up the other gown, Matilda, for I shan't try on any of the rest now — and pray don't bother to stay to help me out of this — I can manage very well alone, thank you."

Matilda, by now quite accustomed to the independent habits of her mistress, withdrew after promising to call Emma within the hour.

After the maid had gone, Emma quickly slipped out of the gown, draping it carefully over a chair for Matilda to deal with later. As she did so, her fingers came into contact with a section of the hem which seemed to be thicker than the rest. Possibly this was why the skirt had not seemed to hang properly, she thought; the seamstress must have made some kind of error in her work at that point. She ran her fingers over the section again and heard the faint crackle of paper. She wondered if part of a paper pattern had been accidentally stitched into the material.

Turning back the hem of the garment, she studied the reverse side. She was sufficient of a needlewoman herself to see at once that this part of the gown was not finished off in the style for which Madame Tiffany enjoyed an enviable reputation. About eight inches of the hem was secured only by tacking threads.

Emma stared at the stitching, thinking how very odd it was; then suddenly she fetched her pocket scissors from the dressing table and began to unpick the threads with deft, practised fingers.

When she had finished, she turned back the material to disclose a many folded piece of thin paper.

As she had supposed, part of a paper pattern. Well, perhaps she could spare the unknown seamstress a scolding by finishing off the hem herself. Madame Tiffany did not appear to be a tolerant woman, and Emma knew what it was to be thrown out of employment. She took the paper up and idly unfolded it, then paused as she was about to screw it up.

There was some kind of drawing in ink on it, and not at all the kind one would connect with the making of garments. This looked more like a map.

She carried the paper over to the dressing table, spreading it out and weighing down the edges with two small glass bottles, so that she could study it properly.

Yes, undoubtedly it was a map; a second, more careful scrutiny told her that it was a map of the county of Dorset. But not of the kind that could be readily purchased in the print shops. This one had been etched in by hand and was scattered with a number of different symbols.

After a moment, she found a key to these symbols in the bottom right-hand corner of the paper. With the aid of this, she learned that the upright crosses represented signal stations; the small cones were beacons; the squares showed where supplies depots were situated; while assembly points for Volunteer Cavalry and Infantry were indicated by circles containing the letter C or I. All the defence measures of the county were clearly marked on this piece of paper.

She sat down on the bed rather heavily. What could this mean? This was not just a piece of paper accidentally stitched into the hem of a gown — it must be there by design. But who would want a map showing in detail all the defences of Dorset against invasion?

Who but the enemy?

Then why had it been stitched into the hem of one of *her* gowns? And by whom?

She knitted her brows as she sought for a satisfactory solution to these puzzles. The gown had come from Tiffany's. She recalled the words she had heard Rupert Wynford say last night — "He did put us on to Tiffany, and she's a valuable line—"

A link in a chain of spies, perhaps? Madame's part in the business being to receive maps and other written information from various dubious sources, in order to pass these on to — whom? Rupert Wynford, through the medium of his wife's new clothes? And then, presumably, he would deliver these treasonable items to someone else, who would make the crossing with them to France.

At that thought, she was on her feet and feverishly examining the hems of all the new garments hanging in her wardrobe. She paused at last, somewhat breathless, but satisfied that there were no more hidden communications among them.

She sat down again to consider. She could be mistaken in her conclusions. Surely such a method of conveying secret papers must always be open to discovery by a third person? But when she remembered that the gown had been one of several delivered at the same time, and the fact that she had barely noticed the fault in the hem, she felt less certain of this. It would be easy enough for Rupert Wynford to steal into her room at some time and remove the map, having been warned in advance by Madame Tiffany, no doubt, of which gown to examine. And then all that would be left for her to find would have been a few inches of unstitched material; Madame would have apologised, put the fault right, and the whole affair would have passed off easily.

If Wynford should be an agent for the French and Madame Tiffany's shop a kind of post office for other enemy agents, then obviously he would be unwilling to visit the shop openly without a very good excuse. Emma realised suddenly that one of the ways in which she had been useful to Wynford had been in providing him with such an excuse. He had taken her to Tiffany's almost as soon as they had arrived in Poyntz Ferrers, and — yes, now she recalled this! — had been alone in conversation with the proprietress of the gown shop while Emma had gone with the assistant to be measured. There had been ample time then for plots to be hatched.

She passed a hand wearily across her eyes. Some action ought to be taken about all this, but what was the wisest thing to do? If only there had been somebody in whom she could confide, some known and trusted friend! She thought of Lady Warham and longed to pour her doubts and fears into that kind, maternal ear. But what comfort had she any right to expect once she had confessed her own dubious part in this sinister affair? Lady Warham would surely turn from her in horror, as any gently bred female would.

Kitty Melbury, then? She might not be as shocked at the story of Emma's duplicity, but she was too shallow a female to be capable of giving any sound advice. Besides, she would most likely suggest consulting her husband; and for some reason not quite clear to herself, Emma disliked the idea of admitting Mr. Melbury to her confidence.

Her mind darted hither and thither among her few local acquaintances, considering and rejecting first one, then another. The trouble was that in a situation as serious as this, only a close friend could be trusted, and she had known these people for such a short time.

She wriggled her shoulders in a gesture of impatience. There were no close friends at hand, so she must make a choice somewhere among these acquaintances. The responsibility of keeping her suspicions to herself for any longer was now too great.

Lieutenant Tilley — of course, he was the person she needed! He admired her, which would make him ready to listen to her story; and he was of the type to make light of her escapade, especially when he understood what a desperate fix she had been in when she had accepted Wynford's bizarre offer. As a man on defence work, too, he would be alive to any suspicion of subversive activity and would know just what ought to be done to counteract it.

After reaching this decision, she felt an overwhelming sense of relief. She picked up the map, folded it carefully, and stowed it away in her reticule. It would be best to carry it with her all the time until she could hand it over to the Lieutenant. There would be no opportunity for that at the gathering this evening. She must make an assignation with him for tomorrow and explain everything then. She could only hope that Wynford would be out of the way. Perhaps it would be safer to arrange a meeting with Tilley away from the house, where there was less danger of prying eyes and ears. She reflected for a moment, decided on a suitable rendezvous, then lay down on the bed for what remained of the time before Matilda had been instructed to call her.

The dinner party was a great success. Rupert Wynford was at his most convivial; and Emma, her anxieties allayed by the prospect of soon having someone to advise her, was able to play the part of a relaxed yet conscientious hostess. After the meal was over, the rest of the evening was passed in conversation and a little light music. At one point, Lieutenant Tilley, who possessed a good baritone voice, had been prevailed upon to favour the company with a rousing martial air. Emma was at the piano, and he bent over her in consultation before beginning on his song.

Afraid to miss this opportunity in case no other offered during the course of the evening, she said in an urgent, low tone: "I must see you alone! Can you meet me at ten o'clock tomorrow morning? There's a footpath to Osmington just below the farm — I'll be a little wav along it, out of sight."

His face was very close to hers and she saw by the lifted brow and slightly widened eyes that she had surprised him; otherwise, he gave no sign.

"I'll be there," he replied, quietly, as he straightened up to begin his song.

Emma raised her eyes for a second as a shadow fell across the sheet of music and realised that Rupert Wynford had moved over to stand on her other side.

He was regarding her gravely. How much had he overheard?

SIXTEEN

Emma found no difficulty in slipping out to keep her appointment next morning. Rupert Wynford did not put in an appearance at breakfast and had left no message for her, so she concluded that either he had risen early and gone about his own concerns or else he was for once sleeping late. She strolled past the church and the farm without meeting anyone in the lane and turned along the footpath which led to Osmington.

She had only to follow it for a little way to be quite out of sight of the buildings. She paused then to look ahead but could see no sign of anyone on the path. Over to her right was a small clump of trees; she walked towards this and at once Lieutenant Tilley appeared.

There was an amused look on his face as he took her arm and drew her within the shelter of the trees.

"No need to advertise our presence," he said, looking down into her strained face. "But why so grim, my fair one? There isn't any fear of discovery — unless you were observed coming this way by anyone?"

"No," replied Emma, through dry lips. She was fighting down a sudden, illogical sense of panic. Now that she had someone to listen to her story, she was not at all sure that she wanted to relate it. "No, there was no one about."

"And I suppose you know quite well that your husband won't miss you for an hour or two, or else you would scarcely have suggested this meeting?"

"I haven't seen him at all this morning. He didn't come in to breakfast."

"The brute," he said, smiling down at her. "But so it always is with husbands, I believe. It's left to bachelors to console neglected wives."

Emma did not like his tone. She drew her arm from his grasp, frowning heavily.

"I'm not in the mood for levity, sir. I have something very serious to tell you, if you'll be good enough to listen to me."

"Oh, by all means, my dear, since I've come here for that very purpose," he replied, easily. "But I feel that I must perhaps just give you a little hint that I don't take such matters all that seriously."

Emma stared at him, failing to understand. "What matters can you mean?"

He laughed. "Why, matters between a man and a female, my sweet hen-witted creature! What else? But come, you've teased me long enough!"

He drew her swiftly into his arms and kissed her in an expert manner.

"No!" cried Emma, fiercely, thrusting him away. "How dare you!"

He gazed at her with a puzzled expression. "What's this? Have you changed your mind then?"

"Changed my mind? Do you mean — could you possibly have thought —" She broke off, too astounded to finish.

"What did you expect me to think, you adorable little turncoat? When a woman makes an assignation with a man — and right under her husband's nose, at that! — there's only one thing he *can* think. And it's no use trying to pretend now that you meant nothing by it, just because you've let yourself become scared! I'll soon make you forget all your fears — you'll see!"

He took her into a firm embrace, pinioning her arms down at her sides. His lips approached hers; but all in a moment he was seized from behind and torn away from her.

"Rupert!" cried Emma and burst into tears.

There was murder in Wynford's eyes as he aimed a powerful right at Tilley's jaw. Tilley staggered under the blow, but soon recovered, standing his ground. The two men looked at each other for a moment in a silence broken only by Emma's sobs.

"You'll want satisfaction, of course," said Tilley, formally.

Wynford shook his head. "No more than I've had in delivering that punch."

His tone was surprisingly level; but Emma, recovering now from the shock, could see that he was keeping himself on a tight rein.

Tilley raised his brows. "What, no meeting?"

"Do you suppose I want my wife's name bandied about?" replied Wynford, scornfully.

"No need for that — I can always insult you in some way at the Club, in front of witnesses."

"Pah! Such shifts won't fadge, as you must know. Your — gallantries — to my wife won't have entirely escaped notice. People gossip — I shan't give 'em the chance. This is the end of the affair. That's all."

Tilley shrugged. "As you wish. Must say you're a deuced odd chap, Wynford. Suppose I owe you an apology, though." He fingered his jaw. "Punishing right you've got there — I suppose I deserve it."

Emma, drying her eyes on her handkerchief and feeling thoroughly ashamed of her outburst, broke in at this point.

"No, that's not quite true. You see, Rupert —" she used his name again, scarcely realising that she had done so — "it was I who asked Lieutenant Tilley to meet me here. But not —"

"Very good of you, ma'am," put in Tilley, quickly. "But I can stand buff for my own actions. Pay no heed to her, Wynford — disordered nerves — not surprising. All my fault, of course. Regret it — very much."

"Yes, well," Wynford said, calmly, "I don't think we need prolong this uncomfortable scene. No doubt you'll wish to be on your way, Tilley."

"Just so." The Lieutenant bowed, turned on his heel and went striding off along the path in the direction of Osmington.

Left alone, Emma and Wynford regarded each other in silence.

"My warning came too late, then?" he asked her suddenly. "Your feelings were so strong that you flung all discretion to the winds? Don't deny it —" as she started to speak — "I overheard you yesterday evening, you know." His tone changed to one of infinite compassion. "My poor Emma! But there is nothing to be done, as I told you before."

The unexpected gentleness of his manner brought Emma very close to tears again. She blinked resolutely, shaking her head.

"You don't understand — it wasn't like that at all —"

"Then why else did you make an assignation with him?"

She could find no way to answer this, so shook her head again.

"Come," he said, gently, offering her his arm. "Let us go back to the house. Don't think I mean to pester you with questions — as far as I'm concerned, the matter is ended and I shall never refer to it again. As for you —" he sighed — "well, you know best about that."

She wanted to tell him that Tilley meant nothing to her but was perplexed how to do this without revealing the real reason for the assignation. As she could think of no plausible alternative to the truth, she kept silent, and they walked back to the house without another word said on either side.

He was met by Burton in the hall, and after a brief low-toned colloquy they left the house together. Emma went slowly upstairs to her bedchamber to remove her bonnet, which was somewhat crumpled from her recent encounter with Lieutenant Tilley.

She found Matilda there, busy about her daily task of looking over her mistress's wardrobe for garments in need of repair, cleaning, or pressing. The abigail bobbed a curtsey and asked if she should leave Emma alone.

"No, thank you, Matilda, there's no need. I only wish to remove my bonnet and tidy my hair — I shan't be more than a few minutes."

Matilda eyed the bonnet dubiously, but made no comment, suddenly recalling another matter.

"Oh, ma'am, you remember the new gown you was trying on yesterday — the pink muslin? You said you thought the hem was wrong somewhere —"

Emma realised suddenly that Matilda would have found the hem unpicked on the gown during the routine inspection and must be wondering about it.

"Why, yes," she replied casually. "I unpicked the stitching myself, but I couldn't find the fault in it. I was by far too tired to bother further, so I'm afraid I left it as it was."

Matilda looked reproachful. "Why, ma'am, there's no need for you to trouble yourself with suchlike things — I'd have done it for you in a trice, but for you saying that Madame Whatsit could do it. Which to be sure she is doing now, being as she sent a girl here not an hour agone to fetch it, saying she knew it hadn't been finished off as it ought to have. And she'll let you have it back again tomorrow first thing, without fail."

Emma did not answer for a moment, turning over in her mind the implications of this. It must mean that Madame Tiffany had been certain that the map would have fallen into the right hands by this morning. There could be no doubt that a very good organising brain lay behind these operations — Rupert Wynford's? She sighed; there could be little doubt of that, either.

Matilda watched her anxiously. "Didn't I do right, ma'am, to let it go? Only you did say as Madame Whosit ought to do it, and you wasn't anywhere in the house, to ask —"

"No, no, Matilda," cut in Emma, reassuringly. "I'm afraid my thoughts were wandering — of course you did right. There could be no earthly reason for not letting it go back to the shop to be finished off properly."

But although she did not know it then, there was a reason; and one which was to have a profound effect on future events.

After a long spell of fine weather, rain set in by early afternoon. Emma sat in the parlour, watching puddles appear on the courtyard, and the dismal scene echoed her thoughts. Now that all hope of confiding in Lieutenant Tilley was gone, she did not know what to do next. Should she destroy the map? Or would it be better to keep it to confirm her story when she had thought of someone who might be prepared to believe her, and who would take the necessary action?

She was half persuaded that it would be best to tear up the map; at any rate, it would be safe from enemy hands for the present, and it might take some time for a new one to be prepared. But, on the other hand, that paper was the only corroborative evidence of her story that she possessed. Without it, anyone could be excused for thinking that she was indulging in hysterical imaginings. Especially as — this aspect of the situation had never struck her before — everyone in the neighbourhood believed her to be recovering from a miscarriage, a malady which was known frequently to produce nervous disorders.

Oh, but Rupert Wynford had been clever, there was no doubt of that! The situation in which he had involved her left her very little chance of freeing herself from its coils.

In the end, she decided to retain the paper for the time being, keeping it always with her in her reticule, so that there could be no chance of Wynford or that valet of his stealing it from her. She would even sleep with the reticule under her pillow.

"I beg your pardon, madam."

She had been so immersed in her thoughts, she had not heard the low tap on the door. She looked up, startled, to find Burton, the valet, standing deferentially on the threshold.

"Mr. Wynford requests, madam, that you'll spare him a few moments of your time."

A little flustered, she rose, grabbing her precious reticule from the table beside her.

"Yes, of course. Where is he?"

"Upstairs, madam," he replied, holding the door open for her to pass through.

She shot him a curious glance as she preceded him into the hall. He was so very much the gentleman's gentleman to all outward appearances; yet judging by the evidence of the night before last, he, too, was a spy for the French, as Rupert Wynford was.

She went up the broad staircase a step or so ahead of him, then paused at the top, uncertain where to go. He indicated Wynford's bedchamber. As he tapped on the door and showed her in, she drew a quick breath to steady herself, uncertain what was to come.

"Wait in the dressing room for a bit, will you, old chap?"

Wynford was addressing the valet, who had carefully closed the door of the room behind him and was now placing a chair by the fireplace for Emma. Burton nodded and withdrew.

Wynford began to stride energetically about the room, in a way not unfamiliar to Emma. She watched him from her chair, wondering what particular storm was brewing. Was he about to refer again to the incident with Tilley, in spite of his promise that he would never do so?

He turned suddenly to confront her. "There's something I must say, and this seemed the place where we're least likely to be overheard or interrupted. Burton is present to preserve the proprieties."

His tone was jerky, his expression hard. Her heart sank. Whatever it was, it was something serious. She forced herself to return a calm answer.

"Very well."

He stared at her in silence for several minutes, a hostile expression on his face. Emma found it unnerving and lowered her eyes to the floor.

He spoke at last, throwing the words at her.

"Who are you?"

SEVENTEEN

There was no time to consider what this might mean, or how best to answer him. Answer she must, and at once.

"I don't understand you." She forced herself to look him straight in the eye with an expression of puzzled innocence on her face. "You know who I am."

He made an impatient gesture. "I know who you are *not!*" he exclaimed, vehemently. "You are *not* Antonia Maleverer!"

So that secret had leaked out somehow. She clenched her hands on her reticule, trying to keep a similar tight grip on her emotions in a desperate attempt to appear unconcerned.

"No," she agreed, calmly. "I told you that it was only a stage name. I am Emma Harcourt — I told you that, too."

"Oh, yes, I'll admit you've been damnably clever!" He came closer, to stand over her in a threatening attitude. "Mixing truth and half-truth to make your story more plausible —" she paled a little at this, wondering how much he knew — "ah, I see that finds a mark, madam! Emma Harcourt you may be, actress you may be — a devilish convincing one at that —" He broke off with a harsh laugh, then continued in a voice rigid with anger — "But you are certainly not the actress Antonia Maleverer who was engaged for this enterprise! That actress is at present playing in the town of Winchester — she has been positively identified by the lady who originally interviewed her in London on my behalf! Now, madam, what have you to say to that?"

Every vestige of colour left Emma's cheeks. Here was the unmasking she had always feared; but now that she knew the meaning of Wynford's masquerade, it was doubly dangerous.

There was only one course open to her — to tell him the whole truth about herself and hope that it would mollify him for the present.

"I see that I must explain everything to you," she said, in a wavering tone. "But pray don't tower over me in that threatening way, or I shan't be able to utter a word!"

He pulled over a chair from the dressing table and sat astride it, leaning his arms on the back and watching her intently.

"Get on with it," he commanded, roughly.

She began her tale, falteringly at first, but gathering confidence as he heard her out uninterrupted.

"When I understood what you wanted me to do," she said, presently, "every instinct urged me to refuse! But my case was so desperate, with no employment, no money and no friends to assist me —"

"Surely there must have been relatives?" he asked, sceptically. "Who was your father — a clergyman, perhaps?"

She shook her head. "No, he was a Major in the Army."

"Was he, b'Gad?" he asked, with quickened interest. "Not, by any chance, the Major Harcourt who was one of Abercromby's lot?"

She nodded, swallowing a lump in her throat.

"I knew him slightly," went on Wynford. "Oh, not well, of course! I was a very junior officer in a different regiment, but it happened that at one time our regiments were stationed together at Brighton. Well, I'm damned!"

"You did say, when we first met that you'd once known a Harcourt," Emma reminded him, "but that you thought it unlikely I could possibly be related to him."

"Yes, well, I believed you to be an actress, then. Although I might have suspected you weren't, come to think of it, when you persisted in behaving all the time like a gently bred female."

"Which I was," Emma pointed out, recovering some of her poise at the turn the conversation was taking.

"Yes, so it appears." He gazed at her reflectively for a moment, then burst out — "Good God, what your sensibilities must have suffered, one way and another! That business of the key —" He broke off, seeing her blush. "Well, I was not to know," he said, defensively. "Naturally, I treated you as what you pretended to be. But I find it hard to credit," he went on, thoughtfully, "that there were no relatives to come forward to assist the daughter of a man who gave his life for his country."

"There was my father's brother," she explained. "I lived with the family for a time afterwards. But my uncle had married a shrew of a woman who never ceased to taunt me with the fact that I was living on their charity; so I took myself off and found a post as a governess. It was very little better," she added, drily, "but at least I was independent. Until I was turned off through no fault of my own, as I have just told you. You must see that I couldn't possibly have returned to my uncle's house after that."

"Yes, I do see." He frowned heavily. "And I also see that if this is the kind of fate meted out to the dependants of England's fighting men, then there is no wonder that some are ready to turn traitor."

"As you have done?"

The words were out before she could stop to think. She would have given anything to recall them.

He sat upright now on the chair, looking at her with an expression she could not define. She sensed a change in the atmosphere, which had become friendlier since the mention of her father.

"Kindly explain yourself." The tone was ice cold.

She threw all caution to the winds — what was there to lose now?

"You are a spy for the French!" she accused, her eyes flashing. "This masquerade was embarked upon to cover your activities — you used me to provide a link with the gown shop in Weymouth, which receives messages from other spies — and also to glean gossip about our neighbours, which might put them in your power! That meeting the other night — I heard enough of what was said to know —"

"Yes," he interrupted, and there was infinite menace in his tone. "You overheard — and not, I think, for the first time? It seems, my dear young lady, that you've been doing a deal of spying on your own account."

"And who wouldn't try to discover what all this mystery was about?" countered Emma, frightened now, but determined to show fight to the last.

"Certainly not a woman who was sent here for that very purpose," he replied, rising suddenly to his feet. "Freddie! You may come in now."

Burton appeared promptly from the dressing room.

"Any trouble?" he asked, looking at Emma.

"Nothing we can't handle, I believe. I've just had the privilege of listening to a most affecting story. Assure you, I could scarce keep the tears from my eyes."

"Every word I told you was the truth!" cried Emma, hotly. "You can prove it, if you wish, by asking Antonia Maleverer!"

"Which will assuredly be done, madam, together with inquiries on one or two other points in your tale," he said, sarcastically. "In the meantime, let us see what you are guarding so carefully in that bag of yours."

He pounced suddenly, snatching the reticule away from Emma before she could prevent him. She jumped up to try and wrest it from him but found herself held firmly in Burton's grip.

"Apologise for treating a lady like this," he said, in a courtly way. "Not my style at all — regret no option, ma'am."

"Fiddle!" snapped Emma, struggling vainly to free herself. "You're no valet, I'll be bound!"

"Must confess, ma'am, have only lately taken to the trade. Used to be a highwayman before," he admitted, confidentially.

"That I can well believe, since I know you both for a pair of villains!" stormed Emma. "How dare you presume to examine the contents of my reticule!" This to Wynford, who was tipping everything out of the bag on to the dressing table. "Kindly return it to me at once!"

He ignored this remark, for he had found the folded paper and was smoothing it out carefully. When he looked up from examining it, his face had paled slightly and his eyes were hard.

"How did you come by this?"

"You know well enough," replied Emma, scornfully.

"Answer me, or b'God I'll —" He took a step towards her in a threatening attitude.

"I found it stitched into the hem of one of my new gowns from Tiffany's — but don't pretend that you didn't know that! It was meant for you, wasn't it?"

"B'God, you've the cunning of the devil!" He looked at her with loathing. "You were about to hand this over to someone else, weren't you? Who was it? Answer, or we'll find ways of forcing the truth out of you!"

A shiver went down her spine as she faced the fierce glitter in his eyes.

"I — I didn't quite know where to take it," she answered, uncertainly. "I thought perhaps Lieutenant Tilley would be the right person, but — but he misunderstood, as you saw."

"Do you think to gull me with that kind of tale? You will have had instructions to pass this on to someone else, and I mean to know the name! Not only that, but also the source of your instructions. Are you going to give me this information voluntarily, or do I have to wrest it from you by means —" the menace was back in his tone — "which I shall regret and you, dear lady, will dislike extremely."

Emma shivered again, this time openly. "Oh, why will you not believe me?" she pleaded. "I don't know what you mean by having instructions from somebody, but I assure you I found the paper quite by accident! One of the gowns — a pink spotted muslin, but that doesn't signify, except that you can confirm this with Matilda, if you like — did not hang well, and I undid the hem to see why! And when I found that what I had thought to be a piece of paper pattern was a map that might be of use to the country's enemies — why, my one thought was to keep it out of your hands!"

The two men looked at her in a silence which lasted for several minutes. It was not a situation conducive to clear thinking, and Emma wondered if she had done herself good or harm by insisting that she was not employed as a secret agent. If only she had been able to restrain that fatal impulse to accuse Wynford of being a spy! It had achieved nothing but to direct his suspicions towards her own past activities; and to make him search her reticule, which she now realised she had been guarding in far too obvious a way. And it had lost any hope she might have had of unmasking Wynford and his confederates. They might make inquiries to prove the truth of her story, to satisfy themselves that she was not part of an organisation; but that would only be to establish the fact that she was the sole threat to their safety. She would never be trusted again — far from it —

What, she wondered with a sudden constriction of her throat, would they do with her?

EIGHTEEN

Emma was forced to endure another twenty minutes or so of agonising doubt. Wynford pushed her roughly into the small dressing room, warning her what she might expect if she attempted to call for help. She knew it was unwise to ignore his threats and doubted if she would be heard by the rest of the household, even if she did.

When the door had closed upon her, Burton looked inquiringly at the other man.

"Well, what d'you mean to do with her? You can't keep her a prisoner in there for long, and it's too dangerous to have her at large."

Wynford nodded. "Must clap her up safe somewhere for the time being. The cottage at Bowleaze Cove, don't you think? You'll stay there with her."

"Oh, Lud, no!" protested Burton. "I bar looking after females!"

"Old Martha will see to her wants — the old girl's safe enough, she's as deaf as a post. But you just keep your eye on madam, Freddie — she's a slippery customer, and we can't afford to have her wrecking our plans at this stage of the game."

"What will you be doing while I'm standing guard over the petticoat?" asked Burton with a trace of envy in his tone.

"Looking into that story of hers. I don't need to tell you that it's vital to our plans to know whether she's working in collusion with others or not. Either way, she's a menace to us at present, so watch her well." He consulted his watch. "I must be off, if I'm to reach Winchester in time for the end of Miss Antonia Maleverer's performance."

"What will you tell the staff here?"

"That she's become unwell again, and I'm taking her into Dorchester to consult a good doctor. I shall warn them that we may be absent for a few nights."

"Won't her maid expect to go with her?" objected Burton.

"We shall be putting up with friends who can't accommodate her," offered Wynford, promptly.

"Brilliant — you think of everything, don't you?"

"No," replied Wynford, grimly. "I did not foresee this difficulty with Emma. But to return to our plan — we'll take the coach, Freddie, and you must drive. When we reach Overcombe, I'll hire a post chaise for Winchester."

"Your plan is excellent, but I can see just one small difficulty. How will you persuade the lady to accompany you without raising the dust among the servants?"

Wynford's face took on an even stonier look. "I shall give her a choice — either she comes quietly, or else I shall force enough brandy down her throat to lend credence to my story to the servants that she's feeling unwell."

Burton whistled. "The devil you will! And do you know, Rupert, I'd thought lately that you quite fancied the girl."

Faced with these alternatives, Emma decided to give them no trouble. Matilda, her face expressive of compassion for her mistress's supposed illness, packed a bag for her. Rupert Wynford, lending colour to the deception, hovered about his wife with a smelling bottle. The coach was brought round from the stables, the luggage safely stowed away, and Wynford handed Emma inside. A few minutes later, they turned out of the drive without anyone at Poyntz Manor realising that Mrs. Wynford was a prisoner.

Emma did not speak at all on the short journey to Overcombe. Her mind was filled with bitterness towards herself. She had made some foolish mistakes, and now she was paying the price of her folly. The worst of these mistakes was that, in spite of the fact that Rupert Wynford was the most despicable of men, she had allowed herself — But here she deliberately cut off her thoughts abruptly.

She had been told nothing of the plans they had made, so it came as something of a surprise to her when Wynford left the coach. He did so before they reached the inn, thinking to avoid any possibility of Emma's raising the alarm there. He went without a word and only one backward glance. She stared after him for a moment, wondering where he was going and if she would ever set eyes on him again.

The coach started forward once more at breakneck speed, and she was forced to cling on the strap to avoid being thrown off her seat. After a short distance, they turned sharp left into a rough lane where the going was even worse. Beside them lay the sea. They had left all human habitation behind when the coach came to a halt before a stone cottage of unprepossessing appearance. Scattered about it were several wooden barns.

A man had come out of the cottage on hearing the coach. He approached Burton and exchanged a few words which Emma did not catch. Then the door was opened and Burton handed Emma down.

"Your lodging, ma'am, for the next few days," he said, apologetically, as he guided her to the door of the cottage.

Antonia had lifted her skirt and was adjusting a garter when a boy of about fourteen years poked his head round the curtain.

"And what the devil do you want, monster?" she asked him, aiming a hairbrush at his tawny head.

He ducked, avoiding the missile with ease, and gave an impish grin.

"Females never can aim straight," he said, disparagingly. "There's a gentleman to see you."

"What kind of gentleman?"

"A gentlemanly gentleman — not a Lord, I shouldn't reckon, but perhaps a baronet. Gentry, anyhow."

"What's he want?" persisted Antonia, wondering if the visitor might be good for a free supper without expecting too much in return.

"Didn't say. But he comes down handsome enough with his blunt," replied the boy, jingling some coins in his pocket. "Taken a rare fancy to you, too — wants to see you very urgent, he says."

"Well, I'll look him over," conceded Antonia, turning away to apply fresh rouge to her lips before a spotted mirror hanging crookedly on the wall. "Show him up, halfling."

He vanished promptly, to return in a few minutes with the gentleman in question. Antonia signalled to the boy to make himself scarce and stood for a moment looking over her visitor with an appraising eye. He was dressed in a well-cut coat of olive-green cloth, fawn pantaloons and Hessian boots which glowed with loving care, but showed signs of recent travel. He had good shoulders, an intelligent face, and keen brown eyes. She thought he looked like a man of action, either naval or military; but there was sufficient humour lurking behind his smile to suggest that he might make an agreeable companion for an otherwise dull evening.

She swept a litter of impedimenta from the only chair in the room, inviting him to be seated.

"Not that I'd trust it overmuch," she said, candidly. "But we Thespians, you know, must take things as we find them."

"I was wondering," he said, "whether I might not prevail upon you to partake of a little supper in my company? There's a tolerable inn where I'm putting up in St. Peter's Street —"

"And where you have a private parlour, I dare say?" she asked, with a roguish look.

He nodded. "But I wouldn't like you to misunderstand me, Miss Maleverer. I came to see you on a matter of business, merely. However, rather than discuss it in these — er — somewhat professional — surroundings, I feel it might be more agreeable to do so over a glass or two of wine in a more relaxing atmosphere. That is," he added, punctiliously bowing, "if you will do me so much honour."

She had an actress's eye for the elegant manner, and she liked his style. What possible business he could have to discuss with her was obscure; but she was an optimist, and it might turn out to her advantage. A free meal was always welcome at any time, moreover, especially when the return expected would be negligible, as he had seemed to promise.

She agreed. They were conveyed to St. Peter Street in a hackney carriage, for which he apologised handsomely, saying that he had travelled post to Winchester, leaving his own carriages in the stables at home.

"And where may that be?" asked Antonia, ingenuously.

"In Dorset," he replied, turning away to give his orders to the innkeeper before leading her into the private parlour.

Something stirred faintly in her memory at the mention of Dorset, but she did not experience total recall until later. When a tempting supper had been set before them and the waiter withdrew, her visitor, who had requested that she should call him Rupert, mentioned a name which set memory in train.

"Emma Harcourt — Emma!" she exclaimed, laughing. "Yes, of course I remember her! Poor child, she was down on her luck when we met — but that's the way it goes, now up, now down, for all of us!"

"Tell me about that meeting."

She stopped laughing, and eyed him shrewdly. "What's your interest in Emma?" she asked, sharply.

He raised his glass to the light and studied the wine it held as though assessing its quality.

"I'll be frank with you," he said, after a pause. "I hope to make her my wife."

"The devil you do!" cried Antonia, in delight. "Well, that would be a splendid thing for Emma. You look a well-breeched cove —" slang escaped her at times — "and I'd say you're a deal kinder than most. Men can be the very devil, but genteel females like Emma need to marry — they're too tender to be thrust on the mercies of this world."

"I don't know," he said, a reminiscent smile playing about his mouth. "She's a regular fire-eater at times, you know. She seems to have a fair notion of how to take care of herself. But that's by the way." His tone altered, becoming brisker. "She's been passing herself off as you," he said, fixing Antonia with a keen look, "and I need to know the truth of how that came about."

"Then why don't you ask her?" she said, bluntly. "She'll tell you the truth, right enough."

"You're a woman of the world, Antonia," he replied, smoothly. "You don't need me to tell you that a man of the world isn't going to build his happiness on the uncorroborated story of what could well turn out to be a designing female. Experience teaches one prudence in affairs of the heart, however worthy the object of one's affections may appear to be."

"True — too true," she allowed. "Well, if you're sure you mean well by Emma — that what I tell you isn't in any way to be used to her disadvantage —"

"Honour of a gentleman," he pronounced, solemnly. "Or if you prefer it, I could swear by Shakespeare and Sheridan —"

That brought a ready laugh, and she began to plunge into the tale. She told it well, with a wealth of gesture and changes of voice tone which brought before him vividly the picture of Emma, pleading with the innkeeper to give her a bed; alone, friendless, cast off with very little money and nowhere to go.

"Where was this place?" he asked.

"The place where she'd been employed as a governess? It was called Marton Hall, and was about a mile from the Crown Inn, where we met. The people's name was Bowyer, I recall."

He nodded, and she continued with the story, even including the details of the borrowed gown and the altered hair style, until she came to the parting between Emma and herself the following day.

"Tell me, did they rumble her?" she asked, curiously. "I'm a fair judge of acting talent, and I believed she might manage to bluff her way through."

"You were quite right — she did. But when I discovered by chance that she was not Antonia Maleverer, she had to confess the whole to me. And so I came to you to find out if what she had told me was the strict truth, or if she was playing some dubious game of her own."

"Such as trying to catch a well-breeched husband?" asked Antonia, with a laugh. "But then for all she could know when she started out for Dorset, all the male members of the amateur cast might have been very much married. She couldn't have counted on coming across an eligible bachelor like yourself — even if Emma had been a calculating type of female, which anyone who's been an hour in her company can see she's not!"

"But it never does, you know, to judge by appearances," he reminded her gravely. "Not for men and women of the world, such as you and I claim to be."

"No, very true," she agreed. "Well, I trust that you're satisfied, Rupert, from what I've told you, that dear Emma is no calculating female, but a gentle, ill-used creature deserving of the best."

He told her that he was satisfied of this; but did not mention that he intended to pursue his inquiries — with the utmost discretion — at Marton Hall.

NINETEEN

To Emma's great relief, she was not locked away in a room of the cottage but allowed to move about freely. The place was small enough; it consisted of a living room and a scullery downstairs, with two small bedrooms up a short wooden staircase leading off the living room. Burton informed her that one of the bedrooms was occupied by the old woman and that the other would for the present be made over for Emma's own use.

"You may do as you choose," he said. "Your abigail packed books and needlework, I believe, among your other things. I regret that no other diversions are available at present. If you should wish to stroll about outside the cottage, there'll be no objection. I'll be there to keep an eye on you, as old Martha will indoors." He hesitated, then added with an air of slight embarrassment — "I'd advise you to accept your present circumstances, ma'am. Harassing females ain't much in my line but needs must when the devil drives."

"The devil," remarked Emma, drily, "being Mr. Wynford, I presume?"

"No end of a good chap, assure you," he replied, awkwardly, "but a deuced tricky situation, don't y'know? Anyway, you try to bear up, ma'am, and don't get resty, and no harm will come to you."

"For how long?" she asked, bitterly.

He shrugged awkwardly and turned away to walk across to the larger of the barns outside.

She asked herself the unanswered question again. Once Rupert Wynford had checked her story, he would know that she was the only threat to his security. It was reasonable to suppose that he would do something to remove that threat.

And yet she could not bring herself to believe that he would go so far as to murder her. She realised now that even in her worst moments of panic, she had never been convinced that he would harm her to any extent. During the past weeks of their enforced intimacy, she had come to know something of the man. He could be hard, ruthless even, in the pursuit of this evil venture of his; but more than once she had glimpsed a softer side of his nature, particularly in his dealings with herself. He must, of course, take some measures to prevent her from meddling in his affairs. She speculated about this; what was he likely to do? Perhaps he would have her taken away to some far distant place. Since he was in league with the French, would he send her to that country? Once there, she would certainly be powerless to return home to interfere in his schemes.

It was not an agreeable thought. Somehow she must find a way to escape from here before Wynford came back. Everything that Burton had said to her strengthened the supposition that no decision would be made about her fate until he did return. But how in the world could she win free when she was under constant surveillance? It was hopeless to try and enlist Martha's sympathy, as the old woman was so deaf that communication with her was impossible except through the sign language which Burton used, and of which Emma had no knowledge. Burton himself — that was undoubtedly a pseudonym, but no matter — was obviously pledged to Wynford's cause and therefore impossible to subvert. That left the other man whom she had seen briefly when they arrived. She knew nothing of him, so how could she set about enlisting his aid? If she had brought a large sum of money with her instead of a few coins contained in her reticule, there might have been some hope of offering him a bribe. But even if she had been carrying enough money, she was unlikely to find a chance of talking to him, as he seemed to spend all his time out of doors.

At least she felt calmer now. But although she racked her brains to think of some plan of escape, nothing came to her. Burton had let slip that Wynford was expected back here tomorrow evening. She looked at her watch; it was almost six o'clock. So early? She seemed to have lived through a lifetime since that scene in Wynford's room, yet it had been barely four hours since. She had only another twenty-four in which to think of a plan of escape and carry it out. The reflection brought back her panic, and for a few moments she struggled hard against tears.

Tears would not help, she told herself angrily. She must find something to occupy her, or she would never manage to maintain her calm. She rose from her chair to fetch a book and her needlework from upstairs. At once, Martha followed her, watching from the door of the bedroom until she had found what she wanted and was ready to go down again. Once Emma was seated quietly in the parlour, the old woman retired to her scullery from which presently came not unpleasant smells of cooking.

Almost an hour later, Burton entered the cottage with the other man, who at once went out into the scullery. Burton remained in the living room, looking uneasily at Emma.

"Very much regret, ma'am," he said, "that I'll be obliged to inflict my company on you at supper. There's but the one room, as you see. Martha and her grandson Tom will make shift to manage out there —" he nodded his head in the direction of the scullery — "but there's no room for a third."

"Please don't disturb yourself, Burton — or whatever your real name is —"

"No harm in your knowing now, that I can see — Frederick Ponsonby, at your service."

He bowed as gracefully as though they had been at a Royal Drawing Room.

Emma inclined her head, an ironical smile playing about her lips. "Yes. May I say it suits you better than Burton? If my memory serves me correctly, it's an undistinguished town. But pray, don't concern yourself over supper, as I shan't be taking any."

"Oh, but no, I say, you mustn't starve, Mrs. — er, ma'am!" he protested, quickly. "I'm sure Rupert would never want that!"

"Why not? It might save him a deal of trouble," replied Emma, bitterly.

He stared at her uneasily for a moment without saying anything.

"The food's not too bad here, y'know," he went on at last, in an encouraging tone. "Simple, of course — a rabbit and onions, very likely, with fish from the local river, and an apple pie. Some of us often come here for a night or two on business, and old Martha's used to catering for our wants. In her younger days, she was cook maid in a good household, so you need have no qualms about eating what she serves up."

"My qualms are quite unconnected with the quality of the cooking, sir. It's simply that I have no appetite for food at present."

"Dare say you think I'm an insensitive noddle-pate," he said, awkwardly, "but it's not so, assure you. I know well enough how you must be feeling. Not much I can say, but one thing — don't think Rupert would ever do you any serious harm. If that's on your mind, you may be easy, ma'am. But best eat something — put you in good heart."

She recognised the wisdom of this; any attempt at escape would require not only all her wits but probably all her physical strength, too. If she did manage to think of a way to evade her watchers, she would have to face a journey on foot over rough ground of almost a mile before she could reach the post road; and who knew how much farther still she might have to travel before she found help?

So when the cloth was laid, she sat at table with Freddie Ponsonby, and did her best to force down a little of each of the courses set before them. As he had said, the cooking was surprisingly good. She speculated about this, and also about the other refinements of life which were evident in this seemingly simple labourer's cottage; a snowy linen cloth and napkins on the table, good quality linen sheets on her bed —

She paused in the act of raising a spoon to her mouth, her eyes glinting with the flash of a sudden idea.

The window of her bedroom was not so very far from the ground that a pair of sheets knotted together might not reach most of the distance. And the sheets were of almost new linen, so they should be able to stand the strain of someone as lightweight as herself. Moreover, the window was at the side of the cottage, with only a blank wall beneath it.

She lowered her eyes quickly to her plate, afraid that Burton, as she still thought of him, should catch the triumphant gleam in them. She allowed her thoughts to play with the idea, examining it carefully. Surely these three would not keep watch on her throughout the night? The woman was old and would need some sleep. It seemed most likely to Emma that they would lock her in her bedroom when she retired and be satisfied that she would remain safe until morning. It was reasonably certain that it would not occur to them to expect her to escape through the window — men tended to underestimate females, thinking them weak, helpless creatures. What an error of judgement!

When the meal was over, Freddie went out into the scullery and she could hear him talking there to Tom. But although she tried hard, she could not follow what was said. Were they perhaps discussing keeping a watch on her overnight? She wished she knew.

She moved aside the curtain to look out of the window. The sky was overcast and darkness was gathering fast. To a certain extent, darkness would be her aid in making her escape, but she wished she could have a lantern to guide her over the rough mile or so of lane that she must walk to reach the post road. Still, there was no hope of that, so she must manage without.

Freddie Ponsonby came back into the room just as she had replaced the curtain and turned away from the window. She was relieved that he had not caught her looking out, although it was unlikely that he could guess from that what was passing in her mind. Still, in view of the dangerous enterprise in which he and Rupert Wynford were engaged, he would be bound to suspect every move she made.

It was with some idea of disarming his suspicions that she accepted his diffident offer of a game of bezique to while away the rest of the evening. He knew that she could play the game, for Wynford had taught her while they were at the house in the New Forest. If she could convince him that she had taken his advice and was now resigned to her captivity, perhaps he would relax his vigilance. So she sat down with him after the cloth had been cleared, doing her best to concentrate on the game as thoroughly as she had done when Wynford had been her partner.

At midnight, she smothered a dainty yawn which attracted her opponent's notice.

"Deuce take it, you must be worn out, ma'am, what with one thing and another!" he exclaimed. They had just finished a hand, and he made a quick reckoning, more from habit than anything else, as they were not playing for money. "There! It works out at about evens — you play a keen game, ma'am, for a beginner."

She thanked him prettily for helping her to pass on the evening. He coloured slightly.

"As to that, the pleasure is mine. Usually play cards here — not much else to do." He seemed about to add something else, then checked himself. "Old Martha went up to bed some time since," he continued, "but you'll find everything you need in your bedchamber, right enough. Regret, ma'am — you must understand these things are necessary — shall be obliged to lock you in for the night. Any emergency, just call out or hammer on the floor. Tom and I will be taking it in turns to sit up down here."

Emma's heart sank. She had hoped that they would both be sleeping in one of the barns, having seen her safely locked up for the night. With one of them always on guard in the cottage, it would be extremely difficult for her to escape through the window; it was too much to expect that she could manage the business entirely without noise, and the least noise would alert the watcher in the room below.

Once in her room, she decided that the only way she could meet this difficulty was to make her preparations straight away. It would be reasonable for her to be moving around the room now, when she was supposed to be getting ready for bed. She tested out the floorboards and found they did not squeak much, except for one over by the door. Those nearest to the window seemed quiet enough, thank goodness. But she must not forget that almost any movement in this room was bound to be heard in the living room below, in a building of this size.

It might be useful to know which of the two men would remain on watch first in the cottage. Having placed her candle on the floor so that it could not betray her, she peered behind the curtain into the night. After a few minutes, she saw the glimmer of a lantern approaching from the nearest barn. That would be Tom. He entered the cottage, and she could hear the low murmur of voices from the room beneath her.

She waited for perhaps five minutes before she heard the outer door close and saw a ray of light cast by the lantern on the ground beneath her window. Suddenly, it swung upwards. She ducked quickly out of sight, remaining pressed against the wall, heart beating fast. After a while, she ventured to take another peep outside, and saw a dark figure retreating towards the barn, lantern in hand. She recognised Burton — or Freddie Ponsonby — by his height and build; so it was Tom who would be taking the first watch.

She set about making her preparations. She stripped the sheets from the bed and knotted them tightly together, testing the knots to make sure they were secure. Then she looked about her for a suitable place to fasten her improvised ladder. There was the bedpost, of course; that was sturdy enough, but the nearest was about three feet from the window, which meant wasting over a yard of her precious lifeline. As it was, she thought this would reach only to within three or four feet of the ground. So far she might manage to drop without injuring herself, but could she be as certain if the distance were increased? It would be an unnerving experience in the dark; and besides, she might make a noise in landing.

Could she move the bed nearer to the window? She looked at it doubtfully. It was a solid oak bed, far too good for a labourer's cottage, and evidently brought in, like so much else, to cater for the mysterious gentlemen who frequented the place. She went to the top end and gave it a vigorous push, but retired somewhat battered from the encounter, having achieved nothing. That would not do.

She cast around for something else. Apart from a chair, which was obviously too light to take the weight, there was only a small wash stand against the far wall. That might answer the purpose, if she could only manage to move it. But how to do so without making so much noise that she would be heard in the room below? There was no carpet on the floor, only a small rug beside the bed, and anything being moved across the bare floorboards would be bound to attract attention.

It was no use; she must find something nearer to the window. She returned there to search the wall desperately for a hook or other strong object to which she could fasten the rope of sheets, but without avail. There was nothing.

Unless … her eye rested doubtfully on the metal strut which enabled the casement to remain open. It was not very thick, and badly rusted through years of use; but it would be possible to tie one end of the sheets there, if only it would hold her weight. There was no other way that she could see.

Before starting on her task, she peered out of the window again. All was dark; no glimmer of light came from the barns. Perhaps Burton had already settled down to sleep there until his turn came for the watch. What of the man in the room beneath? She knelt down to put her ear to the floorboards, but no sound came up to her. He, too, might be drifting into a light doze, ready to wake at the first alarm. It would not do for her to be in too much of a hurry; she must wait a little while — not long enough for the watch to be changed, but perhaps half an hour or so, in order to give Tom a sense of security, so that he would relax his guard.

To her urgent feelings, it seemed the most difficult part of her plan. Every nerve in her body cried out for instant action, to escape now, before anything might happen to prevent her. Exercising iron discipline over herself, she went methodically about her preparations. Treading softly over the floor, she found a cloak among her baggage, and donned it, stuffing her reticule into one of the pockets. Then with fingers which trembled slightly, she began to fasten the improvised rope to the window strut.

It took some time to make the knots firm, as the material was bulky and awkward to tie securely. When at last she was satisfied with the result, she looked at her watch and saw that twenty minutes of the time she had set herself had already elapsed. Should she go now?

Once more she bent down to listen but could hear no sound from below. She thought that perhaps Tom might be dozing — after all, he had most likely been up since dawn, and what else was there for him to do, down there alone? She decided to risk it and gathered the knotted sheets in her arms preparatory to lowering them through the window.

Suddenly she froze in panic, as sounds of movement drifted up from the room below. She strained her ears to try and identify them, but without success. One thing was clear; Tom was not dozing, and it would not be safe for her to go yet.

She dropped the sheets softly on the floor and tiptoed to the bed. As she sat down upon it, it gave a faint squeak which set her heart beating fast. She pushed back the cloak and tried hard to relax. She must wait now for at least a further twenty minutes, she told herself, and then if all should be quiet, she would try again.

Much to her relief, the movements from below ceased in a few minutes and were not resumed. She could hear old Martha snoring in the room next door, but otherwise there was no sound from anywhere in the house. The minutes dragged by on leaden feet. She could feel the tension mounting within her. What if they had arranged to change watch every hour? She would have only twenty minutes' grace once she had reached the ground; for Burton could not fail to see the white sheets dangling from her window as soon as he approached the cottage with his lantern. How far could she get in that time? Could she possibly reach the post road, journeying on foot in the dark, over rough ground?

She remembered with a start that she was wearing her usual flimsy sandals and wondered if Matilda had by any chance packed the half boots which she wore for riding or for bad weather. Raising herself cautiously from the bed in order to avoid another squeak, she investigated, and was relieved to find that the boots were there. She donned them as quietly as possible, reflecting thankfully that she would now be much better equipped to face the walking she would have to do.

She slid from the bed to stoop yet again on the floor, so that she might catch any sound from downstairs. She remained crouching there for some time but could hear nothing.

She decided that she must go now. Nothing was to be gained by further delay. She moved softly over to the window, gathered up the rope of sheets, and slowly lowered it down the wall of the cottage. It was too dark outside for her to be certain of how near to the ground her escape ladder reached, but it seemed to her straining eyes that the distance was only a few feet. She had noticed before that there was grass directly under her windows, so her landing ought not to be too rough.

She stood on the chair which she had placed ready by the window. Now came the worst part. Gulping down the lump of fear in her throat, she grasped the rope of sheets with one hand and the window sill with the other and swung herself over the edge.

As a little girl, she had swung on apple boughs like other children, but she had forgotten how hard the exercise was on hands and wrists. She must remove her right hand from the sill now and transfer it to the rope. But had she strength enough to do it? And would the knots around the window strut take her full weight, if she did?

She gritted her teeth and made the transfer in one swift, panic movement. She felt the sudden tautening of the knots, but miraculously they held. Now she must climb down.

For a few tense moments, she could not bring herself to make any move at all, but hung where she was, just below the sill, clinging on desperately. It was no good, she thought wildly, she could not go on.

The panic passed, and her determination came flooding back; having come so far, she was not going to fail now. Slowly she began to descend, using her feet against the wall to relieve her aching arms of some of the pressure. Once she felt the sheets give, and paused, heart in mouth, hanging perilously in mid-air. But she knew she must go on now. There was no alternative. She scrambled down the rest of the way, came to the end of her improvised rope, looked down briefly to see the ground only a few feet away, and loosened her hold.

She landed sprawling, slightly winded, but unhurt.

She began to run.

TWENTY

Afterwards, Emma never knew how she managed that nightmare flight, stumbling frequently on the rough road, listening always for sounds of pursuit, her heart in her mouth at a score of small, nocturnal sounds. She came at last to the post road and paused for a moment outside the inn; but it was in darkness, and past experience had not encouraged her to seek help at an inn. With no clear idea of where to go for advice and aid in her predicament, she turned along the road in the direction of Preston. She would try Captain Rivers first, as he was nearest.

She could run no longer, but still forced her aching legs to continue at top speed. How long would it be before her warders at the cottage noticed the tell-tale sheets dangling from her window? With any luck, it might not happen for another hour or so. When she had been planning her escape, excessive prudence had made her calculate hourly changes of watch; but it was much more likely that each of the men would take several hours at a stretch.

Heated by the exercise, she cast off her cloak and put it over her arm. A reluctant moon showed now through a veil of cloud; by its light, the road stretched endlessly before her. It was only about two miles to Preston, but that seemed an impossible distance after all she had already endured.

She had not gone far when she heard the sound of a coach approaching from the way she had just come. She glanced apprehensively behind her. Yes, there it was, darkly outlined in the pale moonlight, its lamps winking like twin stars. Merciful heavens, it might be Burton on her track! She must hide quickly — but where?

She looked about her desperately. There was no cover on this side of the road, but a short distance ahead on the right were some bushes. She started to run towards them, but as she did so the cloak slipped from her arm. She caught her foot in it and went sprawling in the road, right in the path on the oncoming vehicle.

Winded and half dazed by the fall, she lay motionless. A good round oath burst from the coachman as he reined in his horses fiercely, bringing them to a halt within a few feet of the inert form. A man sprang down from the coach, leaving the door swinging, and bent over Emma to turn her face up to the light.

"Good God, Mrs. Wynford!" he exclaimed. "What in thunder's name are you doing here, ma'am, like this? Are you hurt?"

Emma sat up, recognising Ralph Melbury. She shook her head but could say no more for the moment.

"Well, we must get you home," he said, briskly. "You're sure you're not injured? Can you manage to walk to the coach, do you think, or should I carry you?"

She shook her head again. "I — if you'll be good enough to assist me, I can manage, I think."

He raised her from the ground, picked up her cloak and placed it about her shoulders, then guided her to the coach. She collapsed thankfully on to the cushions and gasped out: —
"Not to Poyntz Manor, I beg you! Anywhere but there!"

He looked thoughtfully at her pale face and startled eyes for a moment, but made no comment, simply ordering the coachman to drive on. She was grateful for his matter-of-fact acceptance of the situation; for some time, he allowed her to recover in silence.

"Then I suppose," he said, at last, "that I had better take you to my house, where my wife will look after you."

"Oh, please — I'd be so grateful! But there's one thing — I may be followed, they may try to fetch me back — please, I entreat you, sir, could you possibly keep it a secret from everyone that I am with you?"

It was too dark inside the coach for her to see his expression properly, but there was no sign of astonishment in his tone as he answered her.

"I think that can be easily enough contrived. My servants have orders never to wait up for me, so they will all be abed when we reach the house. Only the coachman has seen you, and we may rely on his discretion, I assure you."

"Oh, thank you!" breathed Emma. "Thank you a thousand times! But — but I don't know what to do, or where to turn for help —"

"Suppose you try and tell me what this is all about," he suggested in a calm tone.

She took two or three deep breaths to try and steady herself before replying. "Yes, I believe I must, but I hardly know where to begin. The thing is — I very much fear — in fact, there can be no doubt that I can see — that my — that Mr. Wynford — is a spy for the French!"

He received this astounding piece of news in silence. She began to wonder if in fact he had heard her, when he suddenly said, "What makes you suppose so?"

She sighed. "Oh, it's a long, long story — but I'll do my best to be brief."

She gave him a summary of the events since her meeting at the Crown Inn with Antonia Maleverer. He was a good listener, interrupting seldom, and then only to ask brief questions very much to the point. He seemed especially interested to learn how many other men had been meeting Wynford on the occasion when Emma had overheard their conversation in Wynford's room. Her reply that there had been only two seemed to afford him some kind of satisfaction.

She concluded with an account of her finding the map concealed in a gown from Madame Tiffany's; of Wynford's discovery that she was not Antonia Maleverer, and her subsequent imprisonment and escape.

"If I may say so, you seem to be a most courageous and resourceful young lady," he said, at the conclusion of her story. "But there's no need for you to concern yourself any further in this affair — I myself will see to it."

She gave a heartfelt sigh. "Oh, if only you could know what a weight that is off my mind, sir! But what I can't quite understand is why you appear so little surprised at what I've just told you."

"That's because I'd already begun to suspect something of the kind," he acknowledged. "With all the scare there is concerning espionage, a sensible man notices everything that is at all out of the common way — new arrivals in the neighbourhood, for instance."

This was very much what Rupert Wynford had said, and it made her thoughtful.

"Was that why you asked me so many questions on that evening when we came to your house, Mr. Melbury? Did I say anything then to betray myself?"

"Not specifically, no. You seemed a little nervous of answering me, but then most ladies are often a trifle nervous with men whom they don't know very well. It was later on that my suspicions hardened."

"When was that?"

"Suppose we leave it for the present? You must be very tired, and we're almost there. I shall lead you straight up to my wife's boudoir and leave you there for a few moments while I rouse her. No —" as Emma started a polite protest — "she will not mind, for you need a woman's care, and we can't risk an abigail because of your need for secrecy. Don't distress yourself, ma'am, but leave matters in my hands."

She was more than ready to do this. Now that the need for action had passed from her, she realised how exhausted she was, and longed for sleep. When they reached Mayne House, Ralph Melbury led her quietly upstairs to Kitty's boudoir. They saw no one on the way. He settled her on a comfortable sofa, and she was more than half asleep by the time Kitty joined her, a peignoir thrown hastily over her nightgown.

"You can't stay here for long, Emma," she said, using the forename for the first time in their acquaintance. "My husband says we must take you somewhere else, where no one will think to look for you. But first you'd best come into my bedchamber and make yourself more comfortable — you're covered in dust, poor creature, and there's a scratch down one side of your face. You must have been through a dreadful time!"

Half dazed with sleep, Emma obediently washed her hands and face and made some attempt to tidy her hair. Kitty meanwhile was dressing herself; when she had finished, she went out of the room returning presently with a glass of warm milk which she held out to Emma.

"Here, drink this, my dear, and it will soothe your nerves. We must make another short journey now, but you'll soon be somewhere where you can sleep to your heart's content, for I declare you look ready to drop. I'll just go and get my cloak."

She did not go at once, however, but stood watching as Emma took the glass and drank thirstily. Then she slipped quietly away.

Left to herself, Emma made an effort to rescue stray thoughts from the waves of tiredness which swept over her. The milk — there had been an odd taste about it which was not altogether unfamiliar, if only she could remember... There was something else, too, which had struck a chord of memory — something she had just seen here, and which recently she had also seen elsewhere...

At present, the solutions to these puzzles eluded her tired brain. It was only when she was seated in the coach between Kitty and Ralph Melbury, in the moment before she drifted off into total oblivion, that she suddenly found the answer to one of them.

Exhausted though she was, she had recognised the gown that Kitty was wearing. It was of pink spotted muslin, the exact counterpart of the one in which the map had been concealed.

Emma opened her eyes, coming back from a long distance, and gradually focused them on a lantern hanging overhead. She stared at it for a while, then looked wonderingly about her. Where was she?

She was lying on a bed with a rough blanket thrown over her, in a windowless room with a stone floor. A short flight of steps led up to the only door. She decided that she must be in a cellar.

Pushing aside the blanket, she made an effort to rise, but found her head swam too much. She sank back again, trying to recall the events that had brought her here.

By degrees most of them came back, but she could recall nothing after drinking the milk which Kitty had given her. The taste of that milk … of course, she knew now! It had contained laudanum. She remembered having been given some many years ago to dull the pain of toothache. Had it been intended to soothe her nerves on this occasion, as Kitty had said? A picture flashed back clearly to her mind of Kitty watching as she had drunk the milk. She could see again the curious expression on the other woman's face — wariness, followed by relief as Emma drank deeply, and finally … what? Triumph? Yes, there had been triumph in Kitty's look as she had turned away to fetch her cloak.

But why? What possible reason could Kitty have had for administering the drug to her, if not to soothe her jangled nerves?

Suddenly Emma remembered Kitty's gown, it was evident that both Kitty and herself had ordered the same model from Madam Tiffany. Tiffany had said that Emma was the first client to have it made up, so Kitty must have ordered hers at much the same time. But suppose, she thought suddenly, both gowns were being dispatched at the same time, too, and some muddle had occurred so that she had received the one intended for Kitty — the one with the map stitched into the hem?

She sat up abruptly, her mind clearing with the shock of this reflection. That would mean that Kitty and her husband were working with Madam Tiffany as spies for the French!

But not, she was certain, in collaboration with Rupert Wynford. It was quite clear from everything she had learned both from Wynford himself and from what she had overheard, that Melbury was not trusted any more than the rest of their neighbours.

Surely, though, there could not be *two* sets of French agents in the area working independently of each other? But if not, what was the reason behind Wynford's mysterious activities? She had believed that he was intent on discovering his neighbours' weaknesses so that he might use these to subvert other people to the French cause. But what if there had been another, quite different reason? What if —?

She clenched her hands in an effort to concentrate as she tried to recall details of the conversation she had overheard in Wynford's room that night. "Melbury could be the one Abney was looking for," Wynford had said. Abney — but he had been a French spy. No, stay! The newspaper had said this and everyone thought it likely, but there had been no actual *proof.* Suppose Abney had been nothing of the kind, but some official investigator who had been working in the area and had uncovered Tiffany's guilt, and was seeking her confederates when he was murdered? Could it be — oh, could it possibly be! that Rupert Wynford's strange masquerade was not directed against his own country, but against the enemy? That he had been sent into Dorset to aid Abney in the search for traitors by living among the likely suspects as a seemingly harmless neighbour?

It could be so — dear God, it could be so! Everything she knew could fit such an explanation! She remembered the expression on Wynford's face when he had taken the map from her reticule; it had registered shock before the anger which followed. Yet had he known the map was stitched into one of Emma's gowns, he must have foreseen the risk of its being discovered first by herself or Matilda, so why the shock? Looking back on it now, she realised that he had acted like a man who knew nothing of the affair.

There was something else, too, she had glimpsed for a moment in his eyes before his anger blotted out all other emotions. He had been using anger to cover a deep hurt, though she had not admitted this to herself at the time. What she had known, long before Freddie Ponsonby had told her, was that Wynford would never really harm her. She had been intimidated by the fierceness of his anger, but deep down she had relied upon the bond that had been gradually forming between them without either being fully aware of its strength.

She recalled her dull misery when they had parted on the way to Bowleaze Cove, and how she had wondered if they would ever meet again. Even then, she would not acknowledge the depth of her feelings for him. More than anything she had wanted to believe him honourable, but all the evidence had seemed to point the other way. Persuaded that he was a traitor, she had felt it her inescapable duty to denounce him; but in doing it, she had been tearing herself apart.

And what of him? The incident with the necklace had shown he thought her attractive, but how deep did that attraction go? Did he think of her as a woman whom he wanted for his wife? She recalled his unexpected gentleness and compassion over her assignation with Lieutenant Tilley and wondered for the first time whether such forbearance in a normally quick-tempered man might not indicate a strong feeling of tenderness towards her. And the hurt she had glimpsed in his eyes for a moment when he had found the map — had it been that of a man in love?

What could it matter now, she told herself bitterly, when through her own false assumptions she had placed herself in the power of the very faction which she had thought herself to be fleeing? Where was this place to which they had brought her, and what did they intend to do with her?

She had not long, to wonder. Presently, she heard the grating of a key in the lock, and the cellar door opened to admit Ralph Melbury.

"So you're awake at last," he said, coming over to the bed.

Her mouth was dry, but she tried to pretend she still trusted him.

"Yes," she replied. "What time is it? Have I slept long — I was so weary!"

"Just after six," he replied curtly. "You've slept all day."

"Six o'clock in the *evening*!" she was genuinely surprised at this. "Where am I?"

"In Tiffany's cellar — no harm in your knowing now, though we had to drug you to get you here, knowing you'd never come willingly."

"Tiffany's!" Her eyes widened. "Then I am right, and you are —"

He nodded grimly. "French espionage — yes. So you'd worked that out for yourself at last, had you?"

"It was your wife's gown —"

"Tiffany's one mistake, but it had its credit side, for it showed us where to look for our enemies when the gown returned to the shop without the map sewn into it. We couldn't know then that you were working *against* Wynford —" he chuckled unpleasantly — "but it served as a pointer. And then, of course, you were good enough to tell us all about his mysterious activities."

She said nothing to this.

"I think you could tell me more," he went on. "You mentioned the valet and two other men who came to see him one night — did you hear their names?" She shook her head. "Or the names of any others working with him in this locality?"

"No." With a flash of spirit, she added. "And even if I could, I would not tell you!"

"You're a fool, then. No matter. It might have been useful to know these people for future reference, but our affair here is at an end in any case now that Tiffany's been uncovered. We've been waiting only for dark, then the three of us leave these shores tonight. I regret that you will stay here. There's a notice in the shop window to say that it's closed for good, so it's unlikely that anyone will discover you in time to prevent your unfortunate decease. It's some small consolation to know that through you we shall have avenged ourselves on Wynford for wrecking our plans."

She made a last gesture of defiance. "You're mistaken — I mean nothing to him!"

He laughed shortly. "I know a man in love when I see one — yes, at least we've done something to even the score. Don't bother to shout for help. There's no one to hear you. Adieu, Mrs. Wynford — I mean, Emma."

He turned to go. In a desperate, unthinking effort to escape, she made a rush for the still open door. He caught her easily and was about to lift her and toss her back on to the bed, when a thunderous knocking sounded from above, and a muffled shout came to their ears.

"Open in the King's name!"

TWENTY-ONE

For a moment, Melbury stood transfixed, his hold on Emma loosening. Quickly she slipped from his grasp and dashed up the steps into a dim passage beyond. He was behind her in an instant and seized her roughly just as the knocking broke out again. Footsteps came rushing down the passage from a further flight of stairs which led above; and Kitty appeared, closely followed by Madam Tiffany and a man whom Emma did not know. Kitty's face was pale, her eyes starting.

"Oh, dear God, it's the military — what are we to do?"

He ignored her, speaking instead to the other man. "Look round the back, see if they're there as well! We might make a dash for it down the alley." He turned to Tiffany. "Hold the girl, while I see how many are at the front! We may need her yet, so keep tight hold!"

Tiffany slid a bony arm round Emma's neck so that the least movement would cause her to choke. The men ran off in different directions, returning presently breathless.

"No good — they've a score or more in the alley!" panted the one.

"As many at the front," Melbury replied. "The place is surrounded — they'll be breaking in soon — follow me! I'll take the girl."

He dragged Emma away from Madam Tiffany and pushing her before him, mounted the stairs which led to the ground floor. Outside the door to the showroom, he halted.

"Stay here!" he commanded the others, then kicked open the door and propelled Emma through into the showroom.

The shouts from outside had now ceased; instead, there was an ominous rain of blows from some sharp instrument on the outer door.

There was a curtain across the window of the showroom. Melbury swept it aside and, keeping well behind Emma, thrust her full into view of the soldiers. A shot whistled through the glass very close to her head; she tried to duck, but Melbury held her tightly before him as a shield.

"Hold your fire!"

The command rang out sharply from one of the only two men not in uniform. Emma recognised Rupert Wynford, and a sob rose in her throat.

"You can see we've got your woman, Wynford!" Melbury's shout came to Wynford's ears with unpleasant clarity. "Any shot from you finds her first!" He pulled a pistol from his pocket and held it to Emma's head. "One move to take me, and by God, she gets this!"

Wynford paused for a fraction of a second, his eyes on Emma.

"Don't be a fool, Melbury!" he shouted back. "What good can that do you? Let her go, and surrender!"

"See you damned first!"

His defiant shout rang out just before a loud splintering told that the outer door had yielded to the onslaught.

"Halt! Don't enter yet!" snapped Wynford to the soldiers. They obeyed, standing like cats before a mousehole.

In spite of the tense situation, Ralph Melbury chuckled. They outnumbered him, but as long as he held the woman he could win yet.

"I'll make a bargain!" he yelled. "Let me pass safe to the harbour, and she'll not be harmed! She goes with me, though, until I'm aboard my vessel — I'll put her off in a boat."

Again Wynford hesitated. One wrong move from himself or his men would sign Emma's death warrant. The thought brought out beads of sweat on his brow, but his tactical brain remained cool. Play for time — a situation like this might change in a moment — Melbury only had to move out for a moment from behind the shelter of Emma's body, and a marksman such as Wynford knew himself to be could settle the business without any harm coming to the girl he valued above all else.

"What about the others with you?" he shouted. "We know they're there!"

"You're welcome to take 'em, if I go free!"

There was a rush of feet behind him, and Kitty ran into the room, shouting abuse. Thinking he was attacked from the rear, he automatically swung round and discharged his pistol. Released from his grasp, Emma sank half-fainting to the floor; Kitty's voice stopped abruptly in mid-sentence as she pitched forward on her face, dead.

Melbury just had time to grasp what had happened before a fusillade of shots buried themselves in his body.

It was towards evening of the following day that Emma at last found herself, rested and well on the way to recovery from her recent unpleasant experiences, journeying in a coach with Wynford towards Poyntz Manor. She had spent the night at Captain Gill's house, where the admirably untalkative Mrs. Gill had ministered to her wants. It seemed that Captain Gill had been told such of the facts as were necessary for him to come to Wynford's aid but knew nothing of the mock marriage.

"Thank God you came to no harm!" exclaimed Wynford, as they waved goodbye to the Gills from the carriage. "Although you almost deserved to, beloved little idiot, climbing through windows and God knows what besides! Oh, Emma, I was near demented when I returned to the Cove and learnt that you were in their power!"

His words brought some colour to her rather pale cheeks. "How did you discover where I was?" she asked.

"It was all Freddie's doing. When he and Tom couldn't find you hiding anywhere in the vicinity of the cottage, he guessed that you must have run to one of our neighbours, as you'd no money on you to hire a vehicle or go farther afield. So he made discreet inquiries among the servants —" he broke off and chuckled — "He's no end of a fellow with pretty housemaids, they'll do anything for him! Anyway, he reached Mayne House in the early afternoon to find that Kitty and Ralph Melbury hadn't been in their beds when the servants rose and had been missing ever since. That gave him food for thought, especially as we'd more than one reason to suspect Melbury was the man we wanted. Then Freddie checked with all our men on surveillance, in case they'd chanced to see you. One of those watching Tiffany's shop reported a coach arriving just before dawn, setting down a man and two women. One of the females appeared to be either drunk or ill, as the others had to support her into the premises. Our man didn't know you by sight, of course, but Freddie thought it was a fair gamble that you were the sick female. Oh, Emma!" He leaned towards her, seizing her hands in a strong clasp. "God, I can't bear to think of it! If only I could have got my hands on that swine! Shooting was too good for him!"

"They gave me laudanum," she said. "So it wasn't so very bad — I slept most of the time, until you and the soldiers arrived."

"If ever I knew such a fire-eater!" he exclaimed, as he swept her into his arms. "Oh, Emma, Emma! Only say you'll became my wife in reality — I know I'm not much of a catch — a mere Army Major with a comfortable but not lavish independence —"

"What a pity, when I'd really set my heart on a wealthy Field Marshal," she said, regretfully. "Still, I dare say I shall contrive to make do. But are you an Army man still? I know you once were."

"Seconded to special duties," he said, tilting up her face to gaze into her eyes. "But never mind all that! Do you mean — do you really mean, dearest girl, that you'll marry me?"

"Why, yes, I think I must — I have my reputation to think of," she answered, with a teasing smile.

"Your —" He looked into her eyes again and found his true answer there.

"Oh, stop, Rupert, pray stop! You're crushing me to death!"

After an interval, he slackened his hold and drew her head on to his shoulder, gently stroking her hair.

"I don't deserve you," he said, with unwonted humility. "I treated you abominably, exposing you to so much danger —"

"Well, as to that," Emma confessed, "I brought most of it on myself by running away. It was no doubt stupid of me, but it never seemed to occur to me that you might be a *British* agent."

"You didn't think I could be on the side of the angels? No doubt it was my reprehensible behaviour towards you that gave you such a poor opinion of my character?"

"Well," said Emma, pretending to consider, "you were odious at times, not to say overbearing! But seriously," she added, "I don't think I realised that our country might make use of spies on this side of the Channel. It was a new notion to me."

"Counter spies — very necessary, assure you. But don't let us speak any more of that. How soon can we be married?"

She blushed a little and murmured into his coat that it might be as soon as he wished. After he had expressed a silent, though convincing approbation of this, he suddenly raised his head, saying: "Then I have a plan."

She recoiled in mock dismay. "What, not another of your plans?"

"I think you'll like this one. I'll take you to Juliana's, and we can be married from there. Devon is far enough away from Poyntz Ferrers."

"It's a pity, in a way," she said, having agreed to this. "I love Poyntz Ferrers, in spite of all."

"Well, possibly we'll come back in a few years' time and see if we can purchase the Manor. All this will have died down by then, and our part in the affair will not be noised abroad, you know. Besides, we shall be an old married couple, quite ready to settle down somewhere. Only think of that, Emma!"

She laughed as he held her tightly again. "So we'll start for Devon tomorrow — that's if you feel you'll be sufficiently rested by then, dearest?"

Unable to trust her voice she nodded.

"Capital, for I can't wait too long, my love. And Emma —" with a provocative look in her eye — "perhaps until we do go, you had better lock that door."

A NOTE TO THE READER

It's wonderful to see my mother's books available again and being enjoyed by what must surely be a new audience from that which read them when they were first published. My brother and I can well remember our mum, Alice, writing away on her novels in the room we called the library at home when we were teenagers. She generally laid aside her pen — there were no computers in those days, of course — when we returned from school but we knew she had used our absence during the day to polish off a few chapters.

One of the things I well remember from those days is the care that she took in ensuring the historical accuracy of the background of her books. I am sure many of you have read novels where you are drawn out of the story by inaccuracies in historical facts, details of costume or other anachronisms. I suppose it would be impossible to claim that there are no such errors in our mother's books; what is undoubted is that she took great care to check matters.

The result was, and is, that the books still have an appeal to a modern audience, for authenticity is appreciated by most readers, even if subconsciously. The periods in which they set vary: the earliest is *The Georgian Rake*, which must be around the middle of the 18th century; and some are true Regency romances. But Mum was not content with just a love story; there is always an element of mystery in her books. Indeed, this came to the fore in her later writings, which are historical detective novels.

There's a great deal more I could say about her writings but it would be merely repeating what you can read on her website at **www.alicechetwyndley.co.uk**. To outward appearances, our mother was an average housewife of the time — for it was usual enough for women to remain at home in those days — but she possessed a powerful imagination that enabled her to dream up stories that appealed to many readers at the time — and still do, thanks to their recent republication.

If you have enjoyed her novels, we would be very grateful if you could leave a review on **Amazon** or **Goodreads** so that others may also be tempted to lose themselves in their pages.

Richard Ley, 2018.

SAPERE
BOOKS

Printed in Great Britain
by Amazon